The Journey

A strange coldness swept through me. Not sadness. Not exactly. In a way, I was prepared for this. We had been through so many missions, so much danger. That one of us should die seemed . . . inevitable. Unavoidable.

And then—

Fury.

A wave of fury like a kick to the gut.

I wanted those Helmacrons dead.

Even the book morphs! Flip the pages and check it out!

Look for other ANIMORPHS titles
by K.A. Applegate:

1 The Invasion
2 The Visitor
3 The Encounter
4 The Message
5 The Predator
6 The Capture
7 The Stranger
8 The Alien
9 The Secret
10 The Android
11 The Forgotten
12 The Reaction
13 The Change
14 The Unknown
15 The Escape
16 The Warning
17 The Underground
18 The Decision
19 The Departure
20 The Discovery
21 The Threat
22 The Solution
23 The Pretender
24 The Suspicion
25 The Extreme
26 The Attack
27 The Exposed
28 The Experiment
29 The Sickness
30 The Reunion
31 The Conspiracy
32 The Separation
33 The Illusion
34 The Prophecy
35 The Proposal
36 The Mutation
37 The Weakness
38 The Arrival
39 The Hidden
40 The Other
41 The Familiar

MEGAMORPHS
1 The Andalite's Gift
2 In the Time of Dinosaurs

the andalite chronicles

The Hork-Bajir Chronicles

ANIMORPHS

The Journey

K.A. Applegate

SCHOLASTIC

Scholastic Children's Books,
Commonwealth House, 1–19 New Oxford Street,
London WC1A 1NU, UK
a division of Scholastic Ltd
London ~ New York ~ Toronto ~ Sydney ~ Auckland
Mexico City ~ New Delhi ~ Hong Kong

First published in the USA by Scholastic Inc., 2000
First published in the UK by Scholastic Ltd, 2001

ISBN 0 439 99258 3

Printed by Cox & Wyman Ltd, Reading, Berks.

10 9 8 7 6 5 4 3 2 1

The author wishes to thank Emily Costello for her help in preparing this manuscript.

For Michael and Jake

Chapter 1

My name is Rachel.

And I was facing down a Controller in a purple-and-pink Dunkin' Donuts uniform. He was holding a Dracon beam. Smirking. The little jerk.

Tseeew! Tseeew!

He fired at point-blank range. Hit me right between my two-metre-long tusks.

"HhhhREEEEEuuuhhh!" I roared in pain and anger. Mostly anger. Like a couple of Dracon beam blasts are enough to take down a seven-hundred-and-fifty-kilo African elephant.

Yeah, an elephant. I can morph into animals whenever I want. I can also morph a cat and a cockroach and lots of other animals and bugs. Sounds like fun, right?

Wrong. Like, about one per cent of the time it's not seriously unpleasant. Mostly morphing is a weapon. A weapon in the most desperate battle ever fought by human beings.

Here's the deal. Earth is under attack. The planet has been invaded by aliens called Yeerks. These guys aren't into exploring strange new worlds. They're into exploring strange new bodies. They're parasites. Like lice or ringworm. Only intensely worse.

In their natural state, Yeerks are nothing but grey slugs. Until they infest a host body, enter the brain, sink down into the little crevices, and take complete control.

Once they have you, you can't focus your own eyes, or draw your own breath, or decide when to pee. You are powerless. A slave of the most complete and hopeless kind.

You can still do one thing. Just one terrible thing: you can watch in horror as the Yeerk in your head lies to your family, betrays your friends, plots to take over your planet.

Frightening?

Oh, yeah. And it gets worse.

Me and my friends are all that actively stand between the Yeerks and their evil conquest of humanity. Just a group of five kids and a young alien.

We're trying to hold on until help gets here from a few billion light-years away. See, the

Yeerks have enemies. A race of amazingly advanced aliens called Andalites.

Andalites look like deer. If deer had blue-and-tan fur, humanoid arms, and scorpion-like tails tipped with wickedly sharp blades. Andalites also have two main eyes, on their face, and two on swivelling stalks that sprout from the top of their head. Beautiful and intelligent and cunning.

Not too long ago — who am I kidding, what seems like a lifetime ago — an Andalite ship got fried right above Earth. Torn out of the sky while battling the Yeerks. My friends and I saw it fall. Saw the dying Andalite war prince named Elfangor crawl from the wreckage. Listened — stunned and just a little freaked out — as he gave us the technology that allows us to morph. To acquire the DNA of any animal we touch and then to become that animal. But there was one rule we had to follow: stay in morph for more than two hours and you stay there for ever. Become what the Andalites call a *nothlit*. Stuck in your morph for the rest of your life. Someone who means a lot to me knows about this first-hand. He'd stayed in morph too long and now he lives his life as a red-tailed hawk. He did regain his morphing ability, but when he demorphs he's not a human. He's a bird. The sad part — at least for me — is that he seems to like his life the way it is now.

But even though it seems futile, we've been fighting ever since.

Trying to hold on even though we've just about given up waiting for any more help out of the sky.

So here we are: Jake, our leader and my cousin; Cassie, my best friend; Marco, Jake's best friend and a totally annoying — never mind; Tobias, a lost soul with the body of a bird; and Elfangor's younger brother, Aximili-Esgarrouth-Isthill. We call him Ax.

Oh, there's one important thing I forgot to mention: Yeerks feed on something called Kandrona rays.

The Yeerks' need for Kandrona is the one flaw in their strategy. A weakness, an opening we can exploit. Every three days, thousands of Yeerks gather together at the enormous Yeerk pool complex built under our town.

Destroy the pool and the Yeerks will starve.

We just found out from our android allies, the Chee, that the Yeerks were beginning mass production of portable Kandronas. The heads of the Yeerk organization have had access to these for a while now. But mass production? That meant each and every Yeerk, no matter how low down on the corporate ladder, would be able to feed in the privacy of his or her own home as easily as you nuke a frozen pizza. The Yeerk pool would be obsolete. Our enemies would be rid of their only flaw.

We just couldn't let it happen.

So we'd attacked their factory, a dingy old industrial building on the edge of town, windows painted black. The Yeerks had disguised it as a Dunkin' Donuts bakery. The human-Controllers were even dressed in the ever-so-stylish polyester fast-food uniforms.

The Pepto-Bismol pink polyester did not help my mood. Neither did the fact that we were way outnumbered.

Thirty human-Controllers were working on a crude assembly line in the back of the building. Four more were pretending to make doughnuts up front. There were at least a dozen guards.

I wrapped my trunk around a Controller's waist, tossed my massive head, and let go.

"Ahhhhhhhh!" he yelled, as he went flying. Then—

THUMP!

I didn't see where he landed.

"HhhhREEEEEuuuuhhh!" I trumpeted.

Jake, Cassie, Ax and Tobias were back by the assembly line, on the other side of a false wall. I couldn't see them but the elephant's ears were picking up moans and roars and cries and Dracon beam blasts. Also, something that sounded like equipment smashing to the floor.

Marco was on my side of the wall, in gorilla morph. Three Controllers surrounded him. He

lashed out with his ham-sized hands but the Controllers were slowly backing him against one of the three industrial-sized ovens.

<Marco! I'm on my way!> I shouted.

<Just when I'm having so much fun.>

The Controllers had their backs to me. Didn't see me coming.

I grabbed the middle one. Tossed.

"Aaaahhhhhh!" he yelled.

Now they knew I was there.

The right one turned his handheld Dracon beam at me.

Too slow.

I grabbed him. Tossed.

"Nnnnnoooooo!" he shouted.

Marco moved forward. Knocked the Dracon beam out of the third Controller's hand. Whacked him a solid gorilla punch to the jaw. The guy went down. And stayed there.

Marco and I looked around. Our part of the factory was littered with downed human-Controllers. Yeerks who wouldn't be causing us any headaches for a long, long time.

<Let's bail!> Jake shouted. <Ax says we've got three minutes left to stay in morph!>

I powered through the main entrance, taking most of the door frame with me. Three minutes to demorph or be stuck as an elephant for the rest of my life.

The others were right behind me. Ax in his

own Andalite body. Jake moving fluidly in his tiger morph. Cassie as a wolf, fast and low. Tobias, the red-tailed hawk. And Marco, a gorilla, bringing up the rear.

We ran. Down the deserted alleyway where we'd left our outer clothing. The pavement was damp. Strange misty halos ringed the sodium-vapour lights way overhead.

Not a minute to spare. Crowded in around the stinking rubbish bins and piles of oily, wet rags, we stopped.

<Nice work, guys,> Jake said. <Let's get out of here.>

I focused on my own body, and felt the changes begin.

My tusks went flaccid, like two overgrown pieces of spaghetti. They slurped up into my face, slapping side to side as they retracted.

Morphing is not attractive. Actually, it's pretty much a freak show.

My eyes sort of moved up and down as they travelled from the sides of my shrinking head to the front. Things went blurry for a second until human sight blinked on. And then—

Chapter 2

"Hahooo wwwas that?" Cassie demanded with a mouth that was half-wolf and half-human.

<A small explosion of light,> Ax said. <I believe it is part of a primitive visual recording device called a camera.>

"WHAT?" Marco exploded. "Someone took a picture of me? Not cool. Do you see what I'm wearing? I'm Spandex-boy. Totally not cool."

I heard a rubbish bin tumbling over. Squeaky footsteps on the wet pavement. Someone was running away!

"Everyone stay put," Jake said. "We can't let anyone see us. Tobias?"

<I'm on it.> Tobias flapped his wings and rose up over Marco's head.

"Well, this is great, isn't it?" Marco said.

"We close down a Yeerk-run operation only to let some tabloid photographer sneak up on us. I bet we're on the front page of the *Sun* tomorrow."

"You don't know it was a professional photographer," Cassie argued.

"A kid can hope, can't he?"

"Not funny." Jake, his mouth pressed into a grim line.

One of the reasons we've survived as long as we have is that the Yeerks don't know who we are. They think we're a group of "Andalite bandits".

If they found out we were a bunch of human kids we'd be dead or infested within hours. No doubt our entire families, too.

"I'm going with Tobias," I said grimly.

I concentrated on the bald eagle DNA buried somewhere deep inside me. Demorphing and morphing — especially after battle — is exhausting. But I couldn't just stand around and wait. So much easier to do something. Anything.

The first thing to change was my mouth. My lips bulged out. Grew hard and stiff and turned yellow.

THUD! I fell forward as my legs rapidly shrank. The slimy bricks of the alleyway rushed up at me.

A feather tattoo started at my fingertips and covered my arms in a few seconds. Suddenly, the pattern sprang up and my arms and legs

were covered with actual feathers. The feathers were dark brown, except for the snowy-white ones that replaced my blonde hair and the skin of my face and neck.

My feet split open and formed yellow talons, each of which ended in a hooked claw. Claws that could grab a swimming fish out of a rushing river. My human bones became hollow and light.

Moments later, I was airborne, cruising soundlessly over the deserted streets. I could see the Dunkin' Donuts bakery a few streets away. Rubble spilled out of the door. Nobody was stirring.

The whole neighbourhood was quiet. Which was good. No commando force of Controllers. Not yet, anyway.

There! I spotted Tobias maybe two hundred metres ahead and to my right, flying over some mid-rise buildings.

<Tobias!> I called. <Who was it?>

<Some kid,> he said. <About our age. He had one of those disposable cameras.>

<Where is he?> I asked.

<I lost him,> Tobias said grimly. <He ran into that building with the pigeon cages on the roof.>

<Let's go after him,> I said.

<No sign of him through any of the windows. But it's getting dark and I don't have the best vision for this job at night.>

Neither did the bald eagle. But by then I knew the others were on their way. When Jake felt it was safe they'd morphed owl and followed us. The six of us circled the building, waiting for the kid to come back out or appear in a window. Nothing happened except that the strange mist turned into a steady downpour.

Jake made the call. <We need to keep an eye on this kid,> he said. <But there's no need for all of us to be here. Ax, Tobias, take the first watch.>

We arranged a quick schedule then split up.

I didn't sleep well that night. I spent two hours dreaming I was on the cover of *Time* magazine as a half-human, half-elephant freak. Not exactly the kind of fame that makes Mum and Dad proud.

At three o'clock, I morphed owl and flew back to the apartment building. Tobias and Ax reported that they hadn't seen anything. Cassie and I spent the next two hours flying in endless circles.

Jake and Marco relieved us at five.

I went back to my bed and my nightmares of exposure and infestation.

By eight-thirty Saturday morning, I was awake and heading to Cassie's barn for a meeting. I was tired and grumpy. The weather was rainy and cold. I wanted a nap. Maybe after we got the film.

Tobias was in his usual spot in the rafters. Cassie was mucking out a stall. Marco was sitting on a stool, looking all conditioned and blown-dry. Jake kept yawning. He looked rumpled, like he'd just crawled out of bed. Which he probably had.

Ax was back on watch at the kid's apartment building.

"Let's try to keep this meeting short," Jake said. "I don't want Ax on surveillance alone."

"I don't get it," Marco said. "What was that kid doing all night?"

"Probably sleeping," I grumbled.

<We need a plan,> Tobias said.

"Easy. We steal the film," I suggested.

"That's not a plan, O reckless one," Marco said snidely. "That's obvious. But I'm ready."

Jake nodded. "I spotted the kid around dawn. His apartment is on the fifth floor. The bedroom faces an empty lot at the back."

"Did you see the camera?" Rachel asked.

"I think so," Jake said. "On his desk."

"We get it now," I said. "Before he hands it over to someone or takes it to Photos 'R' Us."

Cassie leaned against her rake. "Probably a hundred people live in that apartment building," she pointed out. "Some of them could be Controllers."

"Yeah," Marco said. "So maybe the kid is in the lift with a neighbour and he just happens to mention these weird creatures he saw in a dark alleyway last night. Before you know it, there's a knock on your door. And it isn't someone with a cheque for a million dollars."

<He could be a Controller himself,> Tobias said.

"We've got to go in," Jake said with another yawn. "We could try—"

ZZZZZiiiiipppppp!

"What the—?" Marco jumped to his feet.

A radio-controlled toy car blew into the barn. More precisely, a slightly damp, pink-and-aqua Barbie 4 x 4. Only instead of Barbie, a very small spaceship sat in the driver's seat. The ship was eight or ten centimetres long, shaped like a baton with two big "engines" at the back and a death's-head bridge in the front.

The ship looked way too familiar.

<Insignificant creatures! Give us the power source and learn to accept your fate as our eternal slaves! We will not crush and annihilate you as we will crush and annihilate all the inferior species of this planet!>

"Oh, man," I said. "You've got to be kidding. Not these guys again."

Chapter 3

O Most Powerful Emperor, Lord of the Galaxy! Bad news. Our ship's engines have again malfunctioned! The treacherous popinjay males pushed the red button instead of the blue one! Weaker and less worthy servants would be vanquished by this disaster! But the brave Helmacron females are undaunted! We alone will capture the blue box of transforming power! All the galaxy shall tremble before us, rightful leaders of our race!

— From the log of the Helmacron Females

Tseeew! Tseeew!

I felt two pinpricks on my neck. Like mini mosquito bites. "Ahhh! Owww!"

Maybe it was the lack of sleep, but I was

already extremely ticked off. I wanted to pop those little jerks.

"The Helmacrons," Marco said with an amazed shake of his head. "I can't believe someone hasn't blasted these maniacs out of the universe by now."

The Helmacrons are a race of tiny aliens. About one and a half millimetres tall, tops. But it's one and a half millimetres of egomania. They sound pretty harmless, right? Wrong. They have this shrinking ray. The technology to make you very, very tiny. To bring you down to their size.

This makes them both annoying and dangerous.

<You would have the Lords of the Universe wait?> the Helmacron voice in my head blustered. <We demand the power source! And we demand it now! Follow our orders and live as our debased swine! Or resist us and be blasted into twisted molecules! See our might. Learn to obey your new masters!>

"I don't get it," Jake said. "We already gave them one jump start. Why are they here again?"

"Who cares?" I asked. "Let's just get rid of them."

"Maybe something went wrong with their ship," Cassie said. "Hey — where are they going?"

The Barbie-mobile backed up, did a 180, and zipped towards the back of the barn.

"Let's go!" Marco said.

We got up and trotted after them. I could hear Tobias flapping above us. We caught up in time to see the truck's rubber tyres bounce off a battered freezer chest in one of the empty stalls.

Jake met Cassie's eyes. "Is it in there?"

"Yes."

"It" was the blue box. That's what we call it. The Andalites have another name for it. Several actually. Anyway, it's the device they use to transfer the morphing power to an individual. Kind of like a super-advanced alien battery. Elfangor used it on us.

Last time we saw the Helmacrons, we made a deal with them. They could use the blue box to power up their engines. Then they had to get off Earth. Pronto. And stay off Earth. For ever.

Obviously, they hadn't kept their half of the bargain.

<They're cutting into the freezer!> Tobias announced.

I couldn't see anything, but hawks have amazing vision. You'd have to have outstanding eyesight to see what the Helmacrons were doing with their tiny energy beams.

Cassie shot a nervous look over her shoulder. "My dad doesn't need to see this."

"No problem," I said. I grabbed a pitchfork that was leaning up against the wall. "I'll get them."

"I'll help." Marco grabbed a ceramic pot. "I'm gonna trap these weirdos like bugs under glass."

We moved towards the freezer.

The pink-and-aqua truck spun around and raced right between us.

Marco pounced.

I pounced and jabbed the pitchfork down on top of the truck. Vaguely aware that my elbow had hit Marco and that he was stumbling backwards, clutching his head.

So what? The Helmacron ship had rolled off the truck and was tumbling towards the freezer. All I had to do was grab it.

Out of the corner of my eye, I saw Marco lose his footing and trip.

"Get it!" Cassie screamed.

"Look out!"

THUNK!

Marco. Sliding down the side of the freezer. Slumping forwards into the hay.

"What happened?" I demanded.

"Marco hit his head on the corner of the freezer," Jake said.

Cassie had already rushed to Marco's side. "Marco? Marco? Can you hear me?"

No reply. He was out cold.

"Man, these Helmacrons are bad news," I complained.

Jake raised an eyebrow. "Rachel, you were the one who elbowed Marco in the head."

"Because the little monsters were distracting me!"

<They're getting away!> Tobias shouted.

I glanced down. The Helmacron ship was right where it had fallen. I picked it up. "No worries," I said. "I've got them."

Tobias swooped towards Marco's head and narrowly missed grazing Cassie with his talons.

"Hey, watch out!" Cassie yelled.

<They're getting away,> Tobias repeated.

Then I got it. The Helmacrons had bailed out of their ship. They were loose somewhere in the barn.

"Where are they?" I demanded.

<Heading straight for Marco's nose!>

"What?" But I was already down on my knees, centimetres from Marco's face.

Frantically, I scanned the hay and earth.

<Move!> Tobias ordered. <Get away from him so I can see.>

Cassie and I scrambled back.

<Oh no,> Tobias said. <This is bad. Very, very bad.>

"What?" Jake demanded.

<They went up his nose,> Tobias said.

"How many?"

<About a dozen.>

<Hah-HAH!> one of the Helmacrons cried. <The vicious human attacks us with a mighty metallic weapon, but we are not defeated! Give

us the power source now and we will kill you quickly! Hesitate and we will prod you with sharp sticks before you die!>

"Give me one good reason why we should cooperate with you pipsqueaks," I demanded.

<Grovel and beg our forgiveness!> the Helmacron demanded. <Do as we say or your oblivious comrade will die!>

"News flash," I said. "Keep threatening us and you'll never get off Earth alive."

<Brave Helmacron females care nothing for their own safety!> the voice shouted. <We care only for glorious victory!>

<As do we, the newly liberated and courageous Helmacron males!> came another voice.

<We will kill the gigantic alien!> the first voice shouted.

<Not if we kill it first,> the second voice answered.

Then the Helmacrons fell silent. Probably beginning their march deeper into Marco's nose.

"What's this about male and female?" Jake asked.

Cassie shrugged. "Don't you remember? When the Helmacrons were here before, Marco and I kind of gave the males a little . . . pep talk. We didn't like the way the females were always bossing them around."

"Yeah. OK. This is a good thing," Jake said.

"Because now the Helmacrons have even more reasons to fight among themselves."

Chapter 4

Marco woke up about two seconds later. He took one look at the three of us staring into his face and got really worried, really fast.

"What happened?" he demanded, rubbing the back of his head and giving me a murderous look.

"Well, not anything good," I said. "Not anything you're going to like."

"What's the matter?" Marco asked.

"The Helmacrons kind of. . ." Jake started.

<You're sort of. . .> Tobias said.

"A hostage," Cassie provided.

Marco's eyes went wide. But before he could ask any questions—

"Ah! Ah! AhCHOOOO!" He sneezed, cupping his hand over his mouth.

"Did he sneeze them out?" Jake demanded.

<I don't see them,> Tobias reported. <Marco, open your hand.>

Marco glared at us and climbed to his feet. "What is the matter with you people?" he demanded suspiciously. "Why are you interested in my bodily fluids? Where are the Helmacrons?"

Cassie came forward and slipped an arm around Marco. "They cleared out of their ship," she said calmly. "And they went up your nose."

"To hide?"

"Well, no," Jake said. "More like — and I'm just guessing — it's because they want to kill you."

"No way!" Marco rubbed at his nose. Let out a snort. "That is so not OK with me!"

"Calm down," Cassie said.

"Calm down?!" Marco bellowed. "I have Helmacrons up my nose! Lunatics! And they want me dead! No, I most definitely will not calm down."

"I just thought we could think more clearly without you shouting," Cassie said.

"Think about what?" Marco demanded. "We have to get them out! They're armed. They might blow an artery or a, a — something else important! What exactly do we have to think about? Do something!"

"We will!" I shouted. "Just give us time to think!"

Marco frowned and flicked at his nose.

"Tobias, you'd better get Ax," Jake said. "First, see if you can get Erek to keep watch for us. He won't be able to follow the kid with the camera if he leaves the building but at least we'll know where he is."

Tobias spread his wings and was gone.

"Can we go in after them?" Jake asked.

Cassie made a face. "Smallest morph . . . I guess a flea is small enough to get into nasal passages. It might be tight, though. Maybe a tick?"

"Ticks are useless in battle," I said.

"Excuse me," Marco cried. "Are you planning to have a BATTLE in my NOSE?!"

"You have a better suggestion?" I demanded.

"No," Marco whimpered, slumping down on a bale of hay.

"Ideas?" Jake demanded.

Cassie sighed. "Well . . . we have the Helmacrons' ship. We could power it up with the morphing cube, get tiny, and go after the Helmacrons as humans. That is, assuming the controls are still working."

Nobody said anything for a few beats.

Considering.

Pretending not to glance at Marco.

I know Marco. Marco is a get-it-done guy. He has the strategic mind of a serious military man and he's never afraid to make unpopular

decisions for the good of the mission. He knew our going after the Helmacrons was the fastest way to solve the problem. He wasn't going to stand in the way of the goal.

Still, we *were* talking about invading his body in an unbelievably intimate way. He had a right to be a jerk about it if he wanted to be.

"That could work," Jake said tentatively.

Nothing from Marco.

<What could work?> Tobias asked.

A red-tailed hawk and a northern harrier fluttered into the barn and settled into the rafters. Tobias and Ax.

"We were just thinking about using the controls aboard the Helmacron ship to shrink ourselves and go after the aliens in Marco's nose," Jake explained.

<Yes,> Ax said. <I believe it is the only way. We have to find the Helmacrons. They have too much information.>

Marco squeaked. "This is so *Magic School Bus*. Rachel, have I ever told you that you could definitely be my Ms Frizzle?"

I ignored him.

"What information?" Cassie demanded.

But Marco had already figured it out. "The Helmacrons know we're humans with morphing power. From what we've seen, the Helmacrons hate the Yeerks and vice versa. But if the Helmacrons learn that Visser Three is looking for a group of morphing bandits, and there was something in it for them, the Helmacrons would sell us out in a minute."

Jake sighed. "OK, we go after them. No choice."

"Isn't anyone going to ask me what I think?" Marco demanded, his arms wrapped around his belly. "The nose you're talking about happens to belong to me!"

Like I said, I know Marco. He'd already accepted the plan.

Jake gave Marco an impatient look. "Well?"

"Oh, sure," Marco said weakly. "Make yourself at home. Just try to be neat. Think of it as the National Nose Land. Keep it in good shape for generations to come."

Chapter 5

Ax fluttered down from the rafters.

Jake nodded. "Tobias?"

<No problem.>

Tobias would keep watch. Let us know if anyone got close enough to the barn to see Ax do his thing.

Ax began to change. His sharp raptor head ballooned up. His bright-yellow harrier eyes migrated to the top of his head, turned blue, and sprouted stalks.

Total freak show.

"Why did the Helmacrons have to show up today?" Marco whined. "I already used my 'Honey, I Shrunk the Animorphs' joke the last time they were around. I just can't get a break."

Cassie went to the freezer and started

digging for the morphing cube. I followed her. Mostly because the sick look on Marco's face was making me uneasy.

"Why does your dad keep a freezer out here?" I asked her.

"We store stuff in it," Cassie said. She handed me an unidentifiable lump of something. It was frozen solid, so cold my fingers started to ache.

"Like what?"

"Frozen grubs," Cassie said, leaning back down into the freezer. "Certain, um, bodily fluids from the animals. Oh, and ice lollies. Dad likes the grape flavoured ones."

"Sorry I asked." I considered the frozen lump in my hand. Decided I didn't want to know.

"I figured nobody in their right mind would go pawing through this freezer," Cassie said. "Besides, I needed a place where no living creature could accidentally come into contact with the cube."

"I'm with you on that one," I agreed.

Ax went to work on the Helmacron ship.

I watched for a while. He used some of the surgical equipment Cassie's dad kept in the barn. Held the precise instruments in his delicate Andalite fingers and carefully manipulated control rods the size of human hairs. Squinting at the procedure for ten minutes was enough to give me a headache.

My eyes kept drifting to Marco. Still sitting

on the hay, looking miserable. I wandered over to him. Sat next to him. Considered giving him a hug, but couldn't quite bring myself to actually do it.

"You OK?" I asked.

"Great. I always wanted to grow up to be a Helmacron Holiday Inn."

It wasn't funny, but I smiled anyway. "We're going to get them," I told Marco.

An hour later Ax was finished.

<This device is very simple to operate,> Ax told us. <The target size has been set. All we have to do is touch this panel and it should engage the shrinking ray.>

I felt wired. Nervous energy. I was anxious to get moving. The Helmacrons had been in Marco's body for over an hour. Plenty of time to do plenty of damage.

"Just show me which button to push," Marco told Ax eagerly.

Jake looked at Marco. "You're going to shrink us?"

"Who else?"

"I thought Ax would do it."

"Isn't he going, you know, on the mission?" Marco asked.

"Well, we know there are at least twelve Helmacrons," I said. "Five of us. Even with Ax they outnumber us more than two to one. I say he comes."

<Operating the device is not difficult,> Ax repeated. <I may be more useful up Marco's nose.>

Marco giggled nervously. "That didn't sound too weird."

Jake looked troubled. "Marco, don't you want to have someone here with you?" he asked.

"You mean, in case I collapse?" Marco asked. "Pass out? Or, to make things crystal clear, drop dead?"

Jake rubbed his eyes. "Right," he said wearily.

"No." Marco shook his head. "If you don't mind, I'd rather have the maximum firepower working to make sure none of those things happen. What's Ax going to do for me here? Hold my hand?"

"We still have the camera to deal with," Jake pointed out.

"I'll handle the kid," Marco said. "One snap-happy loser is nothing compared to a tiny bunch of squabbling psychopaths from outer space."

Jake's expression got serious. "Look, you can't take unnecessary risks while this mission is going on. Don't play hero. Just keep in touch with Erek or whoever he's got on surveillance."

<Prince Jake,> Ax said, <I would also strongly advise Marco not to morph while we are inside his body. As far as I know, this is an unprecedented event in the history of morphing technology. There is no way to predict what the

redistribution of his mass into Z-space and the substitution of a foreign DNA will do to our miniaturized bodies.>

Jake pushed his hair off his forehead. "Got that, Marco?"

"Uh, not really. Ax, try English."

"Look," Jake said. "No morphing, under any circumstances."

"Don't worry," Marco snorted. "The thought sort of makes me sick."

"OK, Ax, you're with us," Jake said. "I'm hoping we won't be gone long. But Marco. . ."

"Yeah, yeah, Erek's phone number is on the fridge. Listen, is it OK if I help myself to a snack after the kids go to bed?"

"All of this strategic planning is fun and all," I said loudly. "But we're giving the Helmacrons a big honkin' head start."

"OK," Jake said. "In the words of my gung-ho cousin, 'Let's do it'."

"We should hold hands," Cassie said. "That way we won't get separated when we shrink. Maybe."

The five of us huddled together. I took Cassie's hand and gently held Tobias's wing. We watched as Marco hovered over the Helmacron ship, looking too big and clumsy.

<Simply place your hand on the panel and pull down the left rod,> Ax said.

"Yeah, I got it," Marco said. "Ready, set—"

<Make sure it is the left rod,> Ax said. <You do not want to touch the right one.>

"I got it," Marco said, sounding annoyed. "Ready—"

FLASH!

A flashbulb brilliance. The light was green and shockingly bright, like looking into an emerald sun. Then, with surprising speed, we all started to get very small.

Chapter 6

Down.

Down, and down, and down.

We were shrinking. Fast.

The Helmacron ship and the blue box were growing larger. Marco was positively enormous.

"Hey, Marco," I said. "From this angle, you actually look tall."

"Hey — cool!"

"Too bad you can't shrink the whole school," I said.

"Ha-ha. And, free this month only, a bonus ha!"

Shrinking is something like morphing an insect. But different, too. When I've been in fly morph the fly instincts feel that being tiny is natural.

Being a teeny-weeny human is just plain weird.

I'd started out at a metre and a half or something. Now I was roughly the size of a Barbie doll. And getting tinier rapidly.

We were the Littles. The Borrowers. Thumbelina and friends.

Marco was peering down on us. His face was the size of a billboard on Times Square. If he'd been wearing Calvin Klein briefs — and nothing else — the illusion would have been complete. Almost.

"Remember, Marco," Jake called. "No morphing."

"What did you say?" Marco asked. "Small people are hard to hear."

"I said, no morphing!" But at that point it probably sounded like, "I said, no morphing."

"I can't HEAR you!" Marco was starting to sound like a cheerleader at one of those televised competitions.

"Tell him," Jake said to Ax.

<No morphing!> Ax yelled in thought-speak.

"OK!" Marco boomed. "Your puny lives depend on my following orders."

That was when the first wave of fear rippled through me.

OK, morphing is creepy. But, in a strange way, you're in control.

Concentrate hard enough and you can control the morph, at least to some extent.

Concentrate hard enough and even when you think you're about to take your dying breath, you can get your own body back.

But shrinking. . .

I couldn't undo this on my own.

In a very real and spooky way, my life was in Marco's hands.

And, of course, Marco was infested with microscopic lunatics that wanted him — and us — out of their way.

Now we were flea-sized, and still shrinking.

The workbench loomed overhead like a windowless skyscraper.

The treads on Marco's trainers were like enormous purple sculptures.

Down.

Down, and down, and down.

Down until rake marks in the dirt looked like hills.

Down until bits of hay were huge, felled trees and grains of dirt were the size of footballs.

And we were still shrinking.

Marco's mammoth form was entirely filling my view. "I just thought of some—"

His voice just blinked out mid-sentence. Like a radio suddenly switched off. But I knew Marco was still talking. I could sense his words as sound waves breaking around me.

Cassie gripped my hand a bit tighter. "What just happened?"

<We are too small to hear sounds,> Ax said.

"That didn't happen before," Cassie said.

<Right,> Tobias agreed. <When the Helmacrons shrunk me and Cassie and Marco, we could still hear. You couldn't hear us. But we could hear you.>

Cassie looked at me. "Something's wrong."

Chapter 7

Marco

Hi, Marco here.

You're expecting some sort of glib remark. A joke, a witty comment. Well, I wasn't in a Jim Carrey kind of mood.

The Helmacrons hadn't exactly charmed me the first time around. Basically, I'd decided they were insane. Now they were *inside* my body.

In there with little unimportant things like my heart and my lungs.

And my friends.

The truth: I was thinking about scribbling out a little note. Telling Jake to take my stereo after I was gone. Explaining to Dad what really happened to Mum. Telling Rachel about the dream where she begged me to marry her.

Adding to the general creepiness factor was

the fact that my friends weren't talking to me.

I heard Ax say, <No morphing!> Then . . . nothing.

Nothing for at least a minute.

Then—

<Marco, this is Ax. We have a problem. You will not be able to hear the others. Just Tobias and me in thought-speak.>

"But you can hear me, right?"

Another long pause. Then—

<Cassie said I should explain that none of us can hear you, either.> Ax, of course.

"Well, how annoying!" I said. "I mean, how am I supposed to keep up troop morale when nobody can even hear my comic genius?"

Nothing.

Oh. Right. They couldn't hear me.

<You need to pick us up and put us in your nose,> Ax said.

Sure. Except — big problem: how was I supposed to pick them up without squishing them? I had to squint just to see them. They were, like, the size of dandruff flakes.

I leaned over and stared at the ground. OK, second big problem: I'd lost them. Frantically, I scanned the dirt and hay. Nothing.

Stupid, stupid, stupid.

I was annoyed. We hadn't thought of this. We should have arranged for everyone to hop on my hand when they got to about a centimetre high.

Because finding my friends seemed totally impossible.

Major feeling of dread.

I'd faced death before. Each one of us had had at least one major close call. But this was different. This was everyone. As in, I would be the only Animorph left alive. Little me against all the bad guys.

I felt like puking.

Stress.

Or . . . something else? Some strange little aliens marching through my . . . what? Nose? Lungs? Brain? Doing who knows what kind of damage.

No time to freak out.

Time to find my friends and stick them up my nose.

<Ahhhhhhhhh!> Tobias suddenly screamed in my head.

My stomach took a lurch.

Definitely stress.

<Marco, now would be an excellent time to remove us from the floor,> Ax said.

"Fine, fine," I muttered. "Just tell me where you are!"

Of course, they couldn't hear me.

Then I saw it. A black bug with a hard shell. Weird pincers in the front. Scary. Considering how panicked Tobias sounded, my friends were somewhere near that big, bad beetle.

I dropped to my knees. At first nothing but dirt. Then—

There!

A few too-colourful grains of sand. I tried to count them. I couldn't smash the beetle if he had one of my friends.

One. Two. Three. Four . . . Five. OK. I reached out and snatched up the beetle by a back leg. Flung him towards the freezer.

<Thanks,> Tobias said shakily.

"You're welcome," I muttered, even though he wouldn't hear me.

OK, I could see the colourful specks. But I still had no idea how to pick them up. And I was afraid to look away.

Chapter 8

Rachel

Our little holiday in the hay forest was nice but I was ready to leave. Especially after the beetle episode.

We could see Marco hovering overhead. His face was an entire landscape. Nose mountain. Cheek plains.

He was a giant.

"Why doesn't he pick us up?" Cassie asked.

Marco wasn't doing anything except staring at us.

"Maybe he's waiting for Jake to tell him what to do," I said nastily. Tiny is definitely not my thing.

Ax looked at Jake. <Prince Jake, it is possible Marco is afraid of hurting us.>

"Right," Jake said. "Let's tell him how to pick us up. Er — how should he pick us up?"

"Easy," I said. "We grab a piece of hay. He sticks it up his nose and we're off."

Jake nodded. "That piece there." He pointed to a piece of hay a few paces away.

Climbing it was easy. At our size the hay looked rough, like someone had taken a cheese grater to its sides. I grabbed a couple of hand-holds and pulled myself up. No problem.

"I feel like I could take on Schwarzenegger," I said.

Cassie nodded as she scrambled up beside me. "Something about being small makes you stronger." We noticed it before. "Like ants lifting a thousand times their weight."

Once we were all aboard, Ax told Marco to pick up the hay. Two fingers the size of redwood-tree trunks lowered, pinched and lifted.

"Ahhhhh!" Cassie screamed.

"Ahhhhh!" I yelled.

We were being blasted into space! The G-force knocked me on my butt. I just managed to hang on. The wind was whipping. I could barely breathe. I saw something flash by. Could have been Marco's knee.

<Slow down!> Tobias shouted.

The wind died down. The landscape beneath us shifted from jeans-colour to T-shirt-colour to chin-colour.

"*Fantastic Voyage,*" I said. "The voyage inside Marco."

<That was an old sci-fi movie. *This* is a horror flick.> Tobias said.

We passed into shadow.

Apparently into — can I just say EWWW — Marco's nose.

When my eyes adjusted to the dimness, I saw a widely spaced forest of rough, textured black hairs, sprouting out of what looked like a waxy, pink granite wall. The hairs were sapling-sized, long, criss-crossing high overhead. A shifting, intermittent wind tossed them.

"OK, everybody off," Jake said. He reached for a nearby hair.

Tobias fluttered above my head.

<Prince Jake, I should morph first,> Ax said. <I think my hooves will slow me down in this "terrain".>

"Do it."

I reached out for a hair and pulled myself on to it. The hair sagged under my weight. Below . . . the void. I could see a bright oval spot of light. I was looking straight out of Marco's nostril. The ground was kilometres away. I quickly scrambled towards the overhang.

Ugh. The wall was oddly warm. Body temperature. There was something really weird about pressing myself into Marco's skin. Gave me a massive case of the heebie-jeebies.

"You know," Jake said thoughtfully. "I think this is the most disgusting mission we've ever done. Something about being inside Marco makes me feel like a Yeerk."

"Check it out," Cassie whispered. "You can feel Marco's breath. In—"

A cool breeze blew up from the opening below us.

"And out—"

Now a warmer moist breeze blew in the opposite direction.

I clung, staring up. The wall arched over my head at a forty-five-degree angle. I couldn't see the end of the overhang, but it went way, way up, disappearing into darkness.

There was no sign of the Helmacrons. No footprints to tell us which way to go.

"Now what?" I asked.

"Climb?" Cassie suggested.

I watched as Ax completed his morph to northern harrier. As his stalk eyes withered and vanished.

SLURP! His tail violently disappeared into his body like an electric cord into a hoover. Tail feathers shot out.

"Let's all get wings," I suggested. "Flying will be easier than trying to rock climb."

Hanging on to delicate nose hairs and the slick wall, we morphed. Tricky, but I felt much, much better as a bald eagle. Touching Marco's insides was freaking me out.

Morphs complete, we put our backs to

Marco's nostril and flew. A red-tailed hawk, a peregrine falcon, a northern harrier, a bald eagle, an owl.

On and on. Like flying into a cave. Darker and darker the deeper we got.

Flying was easier than climbing, but it was still hard work. Each time Marco exhaled, we lost ground. A bald eagle can hover for hours on a nice updraft. But there were no updrafts here. Soon I was exhausted from flapping my wings, up and down.

Before long, a flat plain opened up beneath us. My raptor ears started to pick up sounds.

<Helmacrons,> Tobias said. <Further in.>

They sounded angry. As if they were arguing.

Finally, I could make out their forms.

<Do you guys see what I see?> I asked.

<The Helmacrons,> Jake said.

<Yes, but—> I hesitated, uncertain. Bald eagles see well during the day. They can spot a salmon swimming upstream from a kilometre up. But it was dark now, and I was practically blind. <Isn't something wrong?>

<The Helmacrons look kind of . . . big,> Tobias said.

Kind of big. As in — enormous. Huge. Gargantuan. They were the size of giraffes. No — bigger. Twice as big. As big as air-traffic control towers. I could morph elephant and still only come up to their calves.

Another thing. These were some seriously ugly aliens. Heads: wide and perfectly flat on top. Eyes rolled around up there like big green marbles. Faces: upside-down pyramids. Chins: barbed. Teeth gnashed in from either side of their mouths. And an extra set of legs made them look like walking tables.

<They appear to be exactly a hundred times our size,> Ax said calmly.

<How?> Jake wondered.

<It is possible — perhaps I made a miscalculation when I calibrated the shrinking device.>

Ax? Make a simple mathematical error? No.

<More likely, the Helmacrons guessed we'd try to use the shrinking ray,> I said.

<Guessed — and sabotaged it before they bailed out of their ship,> Jake said.

<The little stinkers,> Cassie said.

Chapter 9

O Great One, Most Courageous of all Leaders, we have bravely marched into a breathing hole of the giant alien! Triumph was within our grasp until one of the treasonable females wallowed in a sticky body excretion! But we, the noble knights of Helmacron, shall overcome this hardship and find the strength to silence the giant for ever!

— From the log of the Helmacron Females

The Helmacrons didn't seem to notice us as we flapped overhead. They were absorbed in themselves. As usual.

<What are they doing?> Tobias said. The Helmacrons were standing in a circle like Boy Scouts around a fire. Only there was a Helmacron where the fire belonged.

<Consulting a map?> Cassie suggested.

<Making dinner reservations?>

<Quieten down, guys!> Jake ordered. <I can't hear them!>

<Why must we delay our glorious mission?> one of the Helmacrons demanded of the others. <A warrior who is stuck and cannot move dies a hero! Should we deprive her of a valiant death?>

I heard what sounded like the rattle of swords. <March on! March on!> several Helmacron voices chanted.

<I care not for our goo-encrusted knight!> another voice said. <But we know not what lies ahead. Perhaps the muck extends through the entire alien!>

<Excuse me,> Jake said. <But what?>

<Goo and muck,> Tobias said. <What little boys are made of.>

<Coward!> one of the Helmacrons shouted.

<Fool!> said the other.

More rattling of swords. I was beginning to think the Helmacrons were going to take each other out and save us a lot of trouble.

Which kind of annoyed me. I mean, I was big-time bugged with the Helmacrons for double-crossing us. It was their fault I was no bigger than a gnat. I wanted revenge! I wanted to launch an attack before there was no one left to attack.

<Eavesdropping is rude,> I said. <Let's figure out how we're going to capture them.>

<I think I've got it!> Cassie said.

<Great!> Jake said. Then, <What?>

<The human nose is lined with mucus,> Cassie said. <Mucus traps dust that floats into the nose. Marco's mucus must have trapped one of the Helmacrons!>

I don't know why she sounded so happy. This whole thing was just so far beyond gross.

<Most animals with lungs have mucus,> Ax said loudly. You wouldn't expect it, but trying to hear thought-speak over the huge debating Helmacrons and the wind was becoming difficult. <Andalites have it, too.>

<Isn't that special?> I said. <Guys, could you focus here? We need to talk attack.>

<Look. It's everywhere,> Tobias pointed out.

He was right. Now that I focused my dim eyesight on the walls and floors and ceilings ahead of us, I could see the snot. Oozing. Dripping. Pooling. Collecting like wax under a candle. Must not have been as thick as wax, though. The wind was blowing up waves on the surface of the pools.

Waves?

<Hey — why is it getting so windy?> I shouted.

It happened suddenly. Gusts of cool, incoming wind. In a totally different rhythm than before.

With my excellent eagle hearing I heard a distant roar. My eagle brain panicked. Wanted to fly. Wanted out of the way of whatever was coming.

Louder!

Now the Helmacrons had noticed.

They were all shouting at once.

<This sudden storm will not defeat the mighty warriors of the Helmacron empire, just rulers of the universe!>

LOUDER!

The human part of me felt a bit jittery, too. The sound was like a freight train closing in on us.

<Get in the snot!> Jake yelled.

<What? No way!>

Jake was already flapping towards the deepest pool. <Do it. Now!> he hollered.

I flew. But it was practically impossible to make progress in the rushing wind. Like flying into the eye of a hurricane. I used all of my strength, pressed my wing muscles to the bone-popping point.

THUMP! And landed in a snot puddle. Stuck.

THUMP! Tobias came in for a wet landing on my right. Stuck.

THUMP! Cassie, further up on the wall.

THUMP! Ax.

The wind hit me like a brick wall. Knocked me off my talons. I landed beak-first in the sticky sea and then started to slide towards Marco's nostril.

Tobias grabbed my talon with his beak.

I stopped just in time for me to see something tumbling towards us. Something big.

A Helmacron!

He, she, it — whatever — was bouncing head over heels like a tumbleweed.

<I shall return!> the Helmacron shouted as the wind tossed him/her into somersaults. <I shall return to force your surrender, vile air-breathing aliens!>

Then he/she was gone.

And so was the wind.

Chapter 10

Marco

I stood in Cassie's barn holding a piece of hay up my nose for about five minutes. Naturally, I felt like a complete idiot. As soon as Ax said it was OK to lose the hay, I dropped it, hid the Helmacron ship, and got out of there.

I'd ridden my bike over to Cassie's earlier, so I grabbed it and started to pedal towards home.

The weather was depressing, grey and overcast and misty. I knew I should probably just go home and hang out in my room. Wait for a message from Ax or Tobias. Mission accomplished. We're heading out.

If Jake and the others didn't show up by dinner time, I'd slip out and contact the Chee. Check on the camera situation. Arrange for some of them to play my friends while my friends were . . . away.

I felt strangely abandoned. Weird when you consider three people, a Bird-boy, an Andalite and a bunch of Helmacrons were holding a convention in my sinuses.

I peddled on. My mind wandered.

Have you ever seen *Fantastic Voyage*?

Dad and I caught it on the late-night movie once. Raquel Welch. Very fit. Anyway, in the film this team travels into the bloodstream of some old dude. The doctors have him knocked out on drugs and lying perfectly still. Supposedly to make Raquel and her posse safer.

Maybe, I thought, *I should go home and lie perfectly still.*

On the other hand, I thought, *if I'm going to kick the bucket, I don't want to go staring at the ceiling of my bedroom.*

I changed directions. Headed towards the industrial outskirts of town, towards the photographer kid's apartment. I had no idea how I was going to get the film. I couldn't morph. Jake and Ax had made that perfectly clear. No unnecessary risks. But I had promised Jake I'd keep tabs on the kid.

I decided a direct approach would be best. Nothing was stopping me from climbing up the fire escape, crawling in through the kid's window and taking what I wanted. Burglars do it all the time. How hard could it be?

I dropped my bike against the wall of an

adjacent building, crumbling and abandoned. Spoke quietly to the filthy homeless man — a Chee — who was watching the front door of the building. Made my way around to the back.

The kid's apartment building was kind of seedy. Peeling paint on the door. Dirty windows. Graffiti. Nobody lived in that part of town because they wanted to. I knew that first-hand.

Maybe the kid was just a kid. Some bored guy who wanted to be a photographer. Well, if that was true it was time someone taught him to stay out of alleyways late at night.

The fire escape descended into an abandoned lot full of broken concrete, weeds and blowing rubbish. A chain-link fence surrounded the lot, but someone had knocked down one of the poles. Maybe hit it with a car. Anyway, the fence was sagging. I walked right over it and stood staring up at the building.

I kept expecting someone to ask me what I was doing. To challenge me. But the whole block was deserted. Deserted at eleven o'clock on a Saturday morning. The windows on the next building were bricked over.

I picked my way over the crumbling concrete to the fire escape. It had a handle, maybe a metre or so above my head. I jumped up six or seven times. Finally caught it. Pulled it down.

CLANKclickCLANKCLANKCLANK!

The rusty fire escape made an incredible

noise as it unfolded towards the ground. OK, maybe breaking and entering in broad daylight wasn't the brightest idea.

I got ready to run. Thought I saw a curtain on the third floor move. But nobody stuck a head out a window. Nobody yelled.

Maybe they thought I was the fire escape repairman.

Yeah, right.

For a moment I considered abandoning this plan. Going home and sitting tight.

I was worried about more than just the local rent-a-cop. The kid could be a Controller. This could be a trap. Yeerks could be watching from the roof, or from the abandoned petrol station across the street. Waiting for the Andalite bandits to make a move for the camera.

I was also worried about police, the ones that weren't Controllers. They don't exactly encourage breaking and entering. Get caught, and I'd be doing time in a juvenile detention centre.

On the bright side, I might be dead before anyone could actually catch me.

And, like Rachel, sitting tight is not my thing.

Unfolded, the fire escape was a wobbly black metal ladder with an even wobblier railing. I put my foot on the bottom rung and started to climb.

Jake had said the kid lived on the fifth floor. I went up, passing a bedroom on each floor.

Floor one: bare futon on the floor. Floor two:

empty. Floor three: flickering TV, empty beer cans. Floor four: stacks and stacks of books. Floor five—

The room was furnished with a metal-frame bed. Tossed sheets. A desk. Empty bag of sour-cream-and-onion crisps. Some notebooks and pens. And . . . a disposable camera.

Bingo.

The window itself was cracked, the frame splintered. I easily hauled the window open with one hand. Stopped. Listened. All was quiet. Bent my head, stepped through, lowered myself into the room. Then—

Click, click, click, click, click.

A sound that was all too familiar. The sound of Euclid, my stepmum's annoying poodle, trying to run on linoleum. The door to the hallway was open. I lunged for it.

"ARF! ARF! ARFARFARFARF!"

CLICKETY CLICKETY CLICKETY CLICKETY!

This didn't sound like a poodle.

OK. I've been a dog. They are basically happy animals. Anxious to make friends. Even the annoying ones like Euclid.

"Nice doggie," I said shakily.

Just then Fido poked his head into the room. He was short and stocky. All shoulders, head, neck. Small eyes. Evil, laughing mouth set with a row of serious teeth. Every one of which was on display.

A pit bull.

An angry pit bull.

"Rrrrrrr," he growled low. A string of drool spilled out of his mouth.

Too far to make a dive for the camera, so. . .

Morph! But I couldn't. Couldn't without the possibility of hurting my friends. Not happening.

That left one choice: run.

I started to back towards the window.

Fido lunged. Jumped.

"Ahhhhh!" I screamed.

Snarling, snapping teeth — just centimetres from my nose! I heard Fido's teeth clank together. Smelled his hot doggy breath.

I put up a hand. "Get away, Cujo!"

Fido sank his teeth into my wrist. He shook his head, sending incredible waves of pain up my arm.

"Get off! Get off!"

Fido shook again.

"Ahhhhhh!" I screamed.

A baseball bat was leaning against a wall. A Louisville slugger. I slid towards it, Fido hanging from my arm like a very ugly charm bracelet. Picked it up with the hand that wasn't being eaten. Whacked Fido across his haunches. Just hard enough to get his attention — not enough to really hurt him. OK, so I'd broken into his home but he didn't have to amputate my arm.

"Grrrr. . ." Fido growled quietly, released and dropped.

I held up my mangled arm.

Fido backed off about a metre, watching me hungrily.

A neat semicircle of puncture holes marked my wrist. A little blood dripped towards my elbow. Bat under my injured arm, I grabbed an old T-shirt off the bed. Wrapped it around my wrist.

Crap. Yeah, I could morph and demorph to heal the injury — except for the fact that I couldn't! Wasn't allowed to. But the pain was pretty intense.

Fido hunkered down and growled low.

Nobody had come running. The apartment must have been empty. Unless Fido's owners were off somewhere calling the police.

I backed towards the window, still gripping the bat. No time to reach for the camera. I had just climbed out when the sirens started. I pounded down the slippery rungs of the fire escape, feeling light-headed.

How do burglars do this? I wondered absently.

I was running across the empty lot when I felt something tickling my nose. I put up my good hand and brought it away bloody.

Chapter 11

Rachel

We pulled ourselves out of the snot.

My right wing was throbbing, hanging loose and broken. I was missing handfuls of feathers.

Tobias hadn't been seriously injured. But Jake's beak was broken, Cassie's neck was twisted at an unnatural angle and Ax was missing half his feathers. We started to morph back to our own bodies.

The Helmacrons were only a few metres away, shouting and screaming like maniacs. They didn't seem too worried about their sneezed-out friend.

<This mission may be more difficult than we thought,> Ax suggested. <We should try to deal with the Helmacrons as quickly as possible.>

<Do you think?> I snapped.

<How exactly can we deal with them?> Jake asked. <They're bigger than us.>

<A hundred times bigger,> Cassie added.

<We have the element of surprise,> I said.

My lips softened as my yellow eagle beak turned into human lips. Talons turned into fingers. I felt a distant itching as my feathers flattened out, and the patterns they made on my skin faded like a bad bruise. I was getting bigger, much bigger. Five of me would have been a whole half a centimetre long.

My broken wing snapped as it twisted and started to grow into a human arm. My insides sloshed and gurgled and turned back into human heart, kidney, liver, lungs.

Suddenly, it was as if someone had turned out the lights. My bird-of-prey vision blinked out.

"Hey," I said. "It's really dark in here."

<That may be—> Cassie's thought-speech stopped as her head became more human than bird. "Another advantage," she continued. "We can morph animals that see well in the dark."

<How do we know Helmacrons don't see well in the dark?> Tobias asked.

"We don't," Jake said grimly.

"I think I do," Cassie said. "Marco and I were inside a Helmacron ship. It was very brightly lit."

<So, we can assume Helmacrons need bright

light to see,> Ax said. <Or, at least, that they do not like the dark.>

Jake made the call: half battle morphs, half creatures that see well at night.

We morphed.

SPROOOT!

Big leathery ears popped from the side of my head.

SPRONG!

My nose stretched until it was longer than my entire body had been. About a whole millimetre. My legs grew massive. Two teeth twisted and grew into curved tusks.

I was at least three times taller than I had been.

A hundred and fifty times heavier.

To the Helmacrons, I was a kitty-sized elephant. Ax, in his own Andalite body, was smaller still. Tobias was a Hork-Bajir at Helmacron mouse scale. Jake and Cassie were fly-sized owls.

<Maybe we should try to channel the Helmacron personality,> Tobias suggested. <They aren't afraid of being small.>

<Maybe they think small is scary,> Cassie said.

<Then they're going to be terrified of us.>

<Now what?>

<Let's try to reason with them first,> Jake said.

<Oh, yeah.> I laughed. <That will work.>

<We don't want them shooting Dracon beams if we can avoid it,> Jake said. <And Tobias, watch those blades.>

We marched forwards until we were standing right beneath the Helmacrons. They paid us zero attention.

Jake addressed them. <Surrender now! Surrender, and we'll let you live as our defiled beasts of burden. Resist us and — and we'll sneeze in your general direction!>

<Very original,> Tobias whispered.

<You call that reasoning?>

<Reasoning Helmacron-style,> Jake explained.

<What are they doing?> I asked, elephant eyes useless in the dim light.

<Looking for us,> Jake reported. <Uh-oh. One of them spotted Rachel. He's pointing his sword at her.>

"Neep! Neep! Neep!" the Helmacrons cheered.

<What's that?> I demanded.

Cassie sighed. <I'm pretty sure they're cheering.>

<Hah-HAH!> one of the Helmacrons crowed. <The insipid aliens fell into our crafty trap! Now they are the ones lacking great size. Victory is before us!>

<Congratulations,> I said.

<Respect us,> Jake bellowed, <or we will tell our friend to bring the wind!>

The Helmacrons started laughing or cheering or whatever that "Neep neeping" was.

One of them took the flat of his sword and knocked me off my feet.

"Neep! Neep! Neep!"

Now, I was getting angry. *Really* angry.

<Jake, this negotiation is going nowhere,> Tobias said.

<OK, go for it,> Jake said. <Minimal damage to Marco, please!>

<Neep this!>

I stumbled to my feet. Ran forwards.

So did Tobias and Ax.

An ugly black Helmacron boot was right in front of us. Ax slashed at it with his tail. Tobias carved with his wrist and knee blades. I stood right on top of the boot.

No reaction.

<Hah-HAH! You think to crush the toe of a brave Helmacron warrior?> the foot's owner hollered in my head. <Your weight is not enough to bruise the *hilna* of a mighty Helmacron!>

I had no clue what a *hilna* was. But I wanted to pulverize some!

I stepped off the boot. Then rammed my tusks straight into it. The Helmacron didn't flinch. He didn't bleed. He was, however, annoyed.

<I will annihilate you, human!> He drew his Dracon beam. His very, very large Dracon beam.

<Uh-oh!> Jake said.

Tseeew!

I dodged.

The beam barely missed me.

Hit the ground.

And then something awful started to happen. Blood began oozing up under my elephant feet.

Marco was bleeding.

Chapter 12

<Stop!> Jake yelled. <Desist, or you will be blown to your doom!>

<Hah-HAH! Helmacrons never surrender! Give us the power source and we will spare your lives. Refuse and we will stop the heart of your comrade!>

<What will that get you?> I demanded. <If you make us mad, you'll never get the blue box.>

<The human in the morph with the elongated nose tries to bluff! She is obviously unaware of our superior intelligence. Perhaps we shall destroy her next!>

<Can they really stop Marco's heart?> Jake asked Ax in private thought-speak that included us and not the Helmacrons.

<Of course. A few well-timed blasts from their Dracon beams could interrupt the heart's rhythm and stop it.>

<From here?>

<No,> Ax said. <They would have to be closer to the heart.>

<How are they going to—>

<Prince Jake,> Ax interrupted. <Perhaps we should offer them what they want.>

<We can't give them the blue box!> I said.

<I agree,> Ax said. <Andalite technology would be particularly dangerous in the hands of these beings. However, I am suggesting we deploy Helmacron tactics. What you humans call a double cross.>

Ax, suggesting something underhand? That made me nervous. Andalites are big on honour and honesty. If Ax was suggesting subterfuge, the situation was even worse than it appeared.

<What's your idea, Ax?> Jake asked.

<Tell them we will give them the blue box,> Ax said. <Get them out of Marco's body. Then do not give them the box.>

<As simple as that?>

<Yes.>

<OK, you win!> Jake told the Helmacrons. <We'll give you the box. Let's go get it.>

The Helmacrons' marble eyes began to roll around madly. <Hah-HAH!> one of them exulted. <This time you bend before the majesty of the

Helmacron superiority! Now you will grovel before your new masters.>

<That's right, we're bending,> Jake said. <Now let's go.>

<Half of us will follow you out of this body,> the Helmacron said. <The other half will stay to guard the hostage and assure that you do not renege on your end of the bargain.>

<No deal,> Jake said. <All of you come with us or we don't play.>

<You think us fools?> The Helmacron sounded miffed. As if we'd insulted her — his? — intelligence. <The time for debate is finished! The time for action is upon us. Brave Helmacron females, follow me to glory!>

With a clanging of swords, the biggest, nastiest-looking Helmacrons began to run away from us. Well, not away from us, but in the direction we weren't.

<Would these jackanapes outrun us to victory?> came another Helmacron voice. <Courageous Helmacron males, follow me!>

More clanging. More running. The smaller, gentler-looking males took off after the females.

<Stop them!> Jake hollered from overhead. <They're heading for some sort of precipice.>

I ran.

Tried to wrap my trunk around a Helmacron's leg and hold him back. But it was like a bunny trying to stop an eighteen-wheeler.

Not happening.

<Rachel! Let go!> Cassie hollered. <They're going to drag you over!>

Over . . . what?

I let go.

Too late!

One of my massive front legs tipped into an abyss. Momentum dragged my other front leg over. I slipped. Fell.

<Agggggghhhhhh!>

I tumbled wildly.

Down, down, down into absolute darkness.

Chapter 13

<Aaaaahhhhhhhh!> I yelled.

Flipping trunk to tail. Over and over. Couldn't sense the bottom. Couldn't sense the shape of the tunnel through which I fell.

<Rachel, it's OK!> Cassie's voice in my head. <You're falling down Marco's oesophagus—>

<Oh, gross!>

<You should hit in a few seconds,> Cassie continued. <Don't panic, we're coming after you.>

Above, beneath, beyond Cassie's voice — a deep, resonating—

Thump *thump*.

Thump *thump*.

The slow rhythm vibrated through me the way the bass guitar does at a loud concert.

Disconcerting. At the same time, something about the rhythm was comforting, like the hum of the fridge in a darkened kitchen.

Also . . . I smelled something. Something that wasn't pleasant. Something sour. Like rotting food. No, not exactly. More like—

Puke!

Oh, man. What else would be in your stomach? Half-digested food mixed with some sort of stomach juice. I didn't even like thinking about the stuff much less—

KER-PLASH!

I went under!

Submerged into a pitch-black sea.

My elephant body started to sink. And then I realized the fluid surrounding me was strangely hot. My leathery skin began to itch. To burn!

Air!

I flailed my big back legs. Rose higher.

I hit something soft with my head. Something that gave under the impact and sprang back.

The side of Marco's stomach? Or the top?

My lungs were burning!

Was there air inside a stomach? Good question. And not one I had an answer to. I had to find the opening I'd fallen through! Somehow get back up. . .

Morph! I told myself.

No time!

I needed air now!

I tried to see above me. Too dark!

Air. . .

I needed air. . .

And then, through the panic, like a vision, came an image from the Discovery Channel. An elephant . . . swimming.

I let the elephant brain bubble up. My massive legs kicked. Slowly, I started to rise. I reached my trunk high, up towards where I thought the air should be.

Yes!

I broke the surface. Sucked air in through my trunk, filling my lungs. Ahhh. . .

Rotten, stinking air. Glorious.

Whoever says TV isn't worthwhile isn't watching the right programmes.

I looked around, dazed and disorientated. My weak elephant eyes more useless than before. But the sounds! Overwhelming sounds. Sloshing. Bubbling. Far away, that low thump *thump*. Also — voices!

<Look! One of the aliens has followed us!>

Tseeew!

I jerked sideways.

The Dracon beam shot went wide.

The Helmacrons!

The beam had lit up the air pocket long enough for me to see I was sharing the cavernous space with eight or ten of them. They were huddled together, way off to my left side. To me in my subminiature state, they seemed about a kilometre away.

More media imagery. Now it was the drowning scene in *Titanic.* Only instead of Leonardo DiCaprio and Kate Winslet, this nightmare flick starred a pachyderm and a handful of marble-eyed aliens.

Tseeew!

That wild shot let me see that though the Helmacrons' legs were submerged, the rest of their bodies bobbed above the liquid. Treading water or floating? Couldn't tell. Couldn't see any effort to stay afloat.

I could, however, hear them arguing.

<We must blast through the left wall! That is the path to true glory!>

<Imbecile! Do you think us morons? Only the right wall can feel the sting of the Helmacrons' wrath!>

Tseeew!

Missed.

Tseeew!

Missed.

The Helmacrons' aim was way off.

But I almost didn't care because the pain in my skin was intensifying. Hundreds, thousands of raw nerve endings were screaming madly. The ironic part about all this was that it wasn't the first time I'd been nearly digested. But that's another story.

<Cassie!> I roared. <Where are you guys?>

<We're coming!> Cassie replied.

<What's taking so long?> I asked.

<We had to morph.>

<What's the big hurry?> Jake asked.

<Oh, no hurry. It's just that Marco is digesting me!> I shouted.

<Does it hurt?> Cassie asked.

<Remember in *Batman* when the Joker dropped his enemies into a vat of acid?>

Jake: <I'll take that as a yes.>

Chapter 14

Most Omnipotent Leader! Catastrophe has stuck our ranks! The alien is full of bizarre lightless caverns and caustic fluids! Two of the weaker males have succumbed! But even though some of us are blinded, we are the boldest of the bold! We will march forwards to the beating organ, stop it, and embark on our plan to conquer the universe!

— From the log of the Helmacron Females

I couldn't see my friends by the time they arrived. The acid had splashed into my eyes, eaten away at the vulnerable eyeball, painfully blinding me. But I heard a clumsy flap, flap way overhead. Wings. Bat wings. The perfect morph for "seeing" in the dark.

<Stay away from the acid!> I shouted to them.

Tseeew!

Tseeew!

<And the Helmacrons.>

<Hey, that was close!> Cassie complained. <We've got to figure out a way to take the Helmacrons' toys away.>

<What can you see?> I demanded.

<There's only one way out,> Cassie reported. <We're going to have to go back up the oesophagus. You too, Rachel.>

Great. That meant I had to morph a bird or bat. That meant passing through my human form — and hoping I wasn't burned alive in the process.

I braced myself for a new phase of pain.

<OK, I'm going to morph out.>

<Rachel, try to do it as fast as you can,> Tobias said in private thought-speak.

I began to shrink. My trunk collapsed into my face with shocking, slamming force. I fought to keep my half-formed nose and mouth up in the air.

Vaguely, I was aware of the sound of Dracon beam blasts and my friends' thought-speak voices. I tried to focus on them. Anything to distract me from the blistering agony.

<Prince Jake, I believe we have a problem,> Ax was saying. <I'm not sure we can go back the

way we came. Some sort of circular muscle has closed off the passageway.>

<A sphincter!> Cassie, of course.

<So, we'll tell Marco to open it,> Jake said.

<Think again. That muscle keeps food from travelling up the oesophagus. It's involuntary. Like breathing. Marco can't control it.>

<We're trapped?> Jake said.

<Trapped above a sloshing pool of acid,> Cassie confirmed.

<Something else,> Tobias said. <A couple of the Helmacrons aren't moving.>

<Dead?> Jake asked.

<Digested.>

"Agggghhhh!" I yelled.

My leathery hide had smoothed, softened into human skin. Was I fully human? Must have been, because an intense agony hit me, made me gasp and swoon.

My skin was burning! And it felt like I was being rubbed with red-hot sandpaper. Eaten away by flame and acid. Tightening, as if it were shrinking away from the bone, shrivelling into ash.

I gritted my teeth. *Morph!* I ordered myself. But my brain was foggy with pain. I couldn't . . . concentrate. I was nauseous and sweaty and my heart was beating way too fast.

<Keep going, Rachel!> Cassie cried somewhere far, far away.

<I hear the humans over there!> one of the Helmacrons shouted.

Tseeew!

Tseeew!

Through the incredible pain seeped anger. I was starting to get incredibly ticked off. Marco slowly digesting me, Helmacrons shooting at me. No way was I dying here, like a piece of bacon in a frying pan. And that meant I couldn't pass out. Had to morph.

Bat, bat, bat, I thought.

<Go, Rachel!> Jake called.

Then—

Tseeew!

Chapter 15

<Agggghhhh!> Jake yelled.

KER-SPLASH!

<Watch out, they're shooting at us!> Cassie shouted.

Tseeew!

<I have been hit!> Ax.

KER-SPLASH!

Tseeew!

<Cassie, watch out!> Tobias called.

KER-SPLASH!

Tseeew!

KER-SPLASH!

<Aaaaahhhhh!> Cassie yelled.

<Aaaaahhhhh!> Jake yelled.

<Aaaaahhhhh!> Tobias yelled.

<Aaaaahhhhh!> Ax yelled.

“What is going on?> I asked foggily. But I could see. They were demorphing. Cassie quickly. The other three more slowly.

<Don’t—> Cassie yelled as her human lips and teeth began to form. “Morph!”

“What!” I screamed wildly, kicking to keep my face above the acid, desperately chanting *Bat, bat, bat* in my head. “My skin is bubbling off!”

“Give me a second,” Cassie grunted in a strange, pain-filled voice. “Then, climb on my back.”

Cassie was growing. In the weird red half-light, it looked as if a rock were rising out of the churning liquid. And then the rock was twice my size. Then double that. Bigger and bigger.

Cassie was going humpback whale.

Our own personal aircraft carrier appearing out of the sea. Maybe not impervious to the acid, but tougher-skinned than a human.

Now fully human, Jake crawled on to Cassie’s still growing back. Then he leaned down and pulled me up, my raw skin screaming at his touch. I lay back, gasping. Tobias was back in hawk form. He took to the air, hovering over us. Ax’s hooves and weak Andalite arms weren’t much use on the slippery back of the whale, so Jake held on to him.

<I am beginning to think this mission was foolish,> Ax said, glancing with stalk eyes at the

patch of burned fur on his hindquarters. <Marco's body seems to be doing an excellent job of defending itself.>

<Against us,> Cassie said.

"Two more of the Helmacrons are dead?" I asked, lips and teeth and tongue about the only part of me not fried. "And excuse me while I try to morph and demorph to get whole," I added.

"Yeah," Jake answered, still panting. "Two more down."

"*Arrivederci* and goodbye," I said bitterly. And then the changes began. Didn't matter what I became. So I chose grizzly. Just to feel like I hadn't been totally defeated.

<Well, not dead, exactly,> Ax said now. <Remember, Visser Three told us the Helmacrons are fungible. Kill one, and his mind is absorbed by the rest of the species.>

<Whatever,> Jake said. <The good thing is they're not shooting at us.>

Tseeew!

Tseeew!

<Ouch!> Cassie said. <The bad thing is that you're wrong. And that I'm an awfully big target.>

<We've got to get out of here,> I said. Briefly bear and a little less horrified. <What's the plan?>

<Capture the Helmacrons and leave,> Tobias stated, coming to land on the whale.

"Great," Jake said. "How?"

<Attack,> I said.

"Attack with what?" Jake asked. "We tried. They're armed. We're not."

<Morph shark?> Ax suggested.

"Could work."

<Look out.> Tobias. <The Helmacrons are up to something.>

I squinted into the gloom. All I could see was a bright glow, like a welder's flame. Time to demorph, get some better eyesight.

Tobias took off again, disappearing into the black. A moment later, he was back. <Looks like they're trying to blast through the cavern with a Dracon beam.>

<You mean, blast through Marco's stomach,> Cassie said.

<What's on the other side of the stomach lining?> I asked, balancing precariously on her big, curved back through the demorph. <Where do they think they're going?>

<Should be—> Cassie hesitated. <Um. A blood vessel?>

"Good." Jake sounded relieved. "Then we have nothing to worry about. The Helmacrons wouldn't go into a blood vessel. They're not fish. They'd drown."

<So they're stuck.> Tobias.

"Stuck unless we ask Marco to throw up," I said, gingerly running whole fingers up an intact arm.

Jake nodded. "Which means we'd be vomit, too. Maybe they'll surrender once they realize they're cornered."

<Surrender is better than drowning or frying.>

<Hang on!> Tobias shouted. <One just went into the blood vessel!>

"What? No way!" Jake exclaimed.

"We need to be closer!" I yelled.

Cassie powered her tail and flippers. The rest of us held on, fingers and talons anxiously gripping.

The Helmacrons were gathered around a long slice in Marco's stomach. The slice had closed, the way a cut automatically does. But I could half-see the skin oozing a red liquid.

Blood.

What was happening to Marco? Was he experiencing intense pain? Lying in bed, at home or in a hospital, groaning, expecting a gruesome death?

Whatever, he had to be lonely. And scared. And extremely angry.

"Marco must have the worst case of heartburn in history," Jake said. A joke. But Jake sounded worried too.

The Helmacrons turned away from the opening to face us.

Tseeew!

<Agggghhhh!> Cassie shouted. <My eye!>

"Stop shooting!" Jake shouted at the

Helmacrons. "We can get you out of here. Surrender now before any more of you die!"

<Brave and worthy Helmacrons do not surrender!> one of them yelled. <It is you who must capitulate to us! Grovel, humans!>

"Why?" Jake asked. "Without our help, you'll never get out of this stomach alive. If you refuse to cooperate, you're going to die here."

"Neep! Neep! Neep!" <We will be victorious!> one of them shouted. <And when we rule the universe, we will not spare your lives! Not even so you may scrape our boots!>

The Helmacron stepped forwards. He pulled apart the slice in Marco's stomach. Began to wiggle in through the flaps of skin. Then—

SLLLLLUUUSSSH!

With an awful sucking sound, he disappeared.

Chapter 16

<To victory!>

SLLLLLUUUSSSH!

Another Helmacron disappeared through the stomach lining.

<To glory!>

SLLLLLUUUSSSH!

Another, gone.

<To still the beating organ!>

SLLLLLUUUSSSH!

Another.

Now there were only five left. Four had already entered Marco's bloodstream as calmly as I would step on to an escalator at the mall.

It was horrifying.

<What are they doing?> Cassie asked, trance-like.

I couldn't look away. None of us could. We were exhausted, from the rapid-fire morphing, the acid bath painfest, the utter strangeness of being inside the human body.

We did nothing to stop the Helmacrons.

<Maybe it's a kamikaze mission,> Tobias suggested. <Maybe they don't care if they die as long as they kill Marco.>

"But they're going to drown before they get to Marco's heart!" I said.

"It's suicide," Jake agreed. "Pointless. Crazy. Doesn't make any sense."

<Nothing these beings do makes any sense,> Ax pointed out.

Three more Helmacrons wiggled through the cut. Only two were left in the stomach now.

<To the cowardly heart of the swollen alien!>

SLLLLLUUUSSSH!

That sound. I was going to hear it in my nightmares.

"Will it hurt Marco to have them in his bloodstream?" Jake asked suddenly.

<They should suffocate quickly,> Cassie said. <And then they should be broken down and washed out like any waste.>

SLLLLLUUUSSSH!

The last of the Helmacrons disappeared through the cut.

<Another possibility occurs to me,> Ax said.

"What possibility?" Jake demanded.

<Perhaps our basic assumption is incorrect.>

<What assumption?> Tobias said. <You go into an airless environment, you suffocate. Where's the big debate?>

<The bloodstream isn't airless,> Cassie said. <Blood contains oxygen. The main purpose of blood is to carry oxygen around the body.>

"Yeah, but you'd have to be a fish to breathe it," Jake argued.

<You'd need specialized lungs.>

"How do we know Helmacrons aren't fish?" I asked, knowing in a flash that we'd royally screwed up. "The Helmacron home world could be an aquarium somewhere in Iowa for all we know."

<They walk on dry ground,> Tobias said.

"Maybe they're, you know, those animals that can live in water and on land," I suggested. "Like frogs. Or turtles."

<Amphibians,> Cassie said.

<Or maybe they do not breathe at all,> Ax said.

"How can you be alive and not breathe?" I argued.

Ax blinked his main eyes at me. <Trees are alive and they do not actually breathe.>

"If Helmacrons don't breathe, why do they have noses?" Jake.

<It is possible the organ has another use,> Ax said. <Although it is hard to imagine what it would be.>

"This from a boy who eats with his feet," I said dryly.

Jake sighed. "Are you telling me the Helmacrons we just saw walk through a hole in Marco's stomach aren't dead?"

<They don't really die,> Cassie said miserably. <Fungible, remember?>

"Whatever!" Jake bellowed. "Are you telling me we have to go after them?"

<The Helmacrons' physiology is unusual,> Ax mused. <I observed that they were unusually buoyant in the stomach fluids. It is almost as if they are—>

"Cork," I interrupted.

"Or mushrooms," Cassie said.

Great. So, how do we go after a bunch of mushrooms?"

"Dolphins?" I suggested.

<Dolphins have to surface to breathe,> Cassie said. <And we won't be able to surface in a vein. The only possible morph is shark.>

"Will we be able to breathe in blood?" Jake asked.

<I think so,> Cassie said uneasily. <I vaguely remember hearing some scientist interviewed on the Discovery Channel once. She said plasma evolved from seawater. Plasma and seawater have the same basic properties.>

<The shark's gonna be hard to control,> Tobias said. <We're surrounded by blood, folks.>

"We have to try," I said. "If Marco dies, so do we. We've got to stop the Helmacrons."

Jake raised his eyebrows at me. "That didn't sound too self-serving."

"I don't care if it did," I said harshly. "We've got to survive. The Yeerks, remember? That whole 'save humanity' bit? The Helmacrons aren't the baddest aliens on Earth. Just the most annoying. And remember," I added, "we have no proof the Helmacrons aren't working with the Yeerks this time. Or that they won't decide to in the very near future. In which case, we are very ancient history."

<Rachel is correct,> Ax said. <For all we know, Visser Three put the Helmacrons up to this foolish scheme. Perhaps it is simply a way of diverting our attention while something far more serious occurs in the outside world.>

Silence. If what Ax and I were saying was true, we were finished.

OK, Rachel, block out the fear and deal with the Helmacrons. Now.

"OK, we go shark," Jake said. "But I want everyone concentrating on controlling the morph."

One by one, we tumbled down off Cassie's back.

"Agh." I moaned as the acid hit my fresh, renewed skin.

I heard the others gasp and groan as they hit the liquid.

We began to morph, Cassie to demorph first. Almost immediately, my legs fused together right down the middle. I fought to stay afloat as my legs stretched out and out, forming a long, powerful tail.

Half-girl. Half-fish. Mermaid Rachel.

Then the teeth began to grow. Row after row of small but very sharp teeth. My eyes migrated down to my cheeks. My cheeks exploded outwards, forming a dumbbell-shaped head. The pain of the acid bath drained away as the rough sandpaper skin of the shark grew over my own tender human flesh.

I was almost enjoying the morph. Liked the tough skin. Liked getting bigger.

Then the shark's mind infiltrated my own.

And I completely lost control.

Chapter 17

Blood!

So close!

Find the prey. Kill the prey!

I powered my tail, swam rapidly towards the overpowering smell. Sharks can smell one drop of blood in a vast ocean reeking with life. But *this* smell! So rich, so strong.

I turned tightly. Poked my strange head into a tight opening and pushed through.

A narrow space. A few centimetres on one side. A few centimetres on the other. The shark didn't care. Sharks have no fear.

And the smell! So much blood!

I swam with the current, crossing frantically from one side of the confining space to the other. The prey — where was it? I was confused.

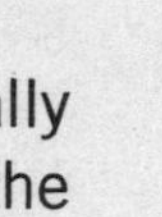

I should see the prey silhouetted against the sunlight above.

But there was no sunlight.

And the blood was everywhere!

Imagine a drug addict awash in a sea of drugs.

Ax anywhere *near* cinnamon buns.

The prey is here! the shark brain shouted. *It's everywhere!* But . . . where?

The shark could hear a low thump, *thump*. The stomach gurgling. It could see walls sloping above, sloping below. Contracting and expanding ever so slightly.

The shark could sense the electricity given off by other living things. Could sense a strong, surrounding hum. And four more weaker pulses.

I twisted my head, spinning my entire body in the process.

There!

A shark surrounded by, immersed in, blood!

Prey.

I attacked!

Lunged with my huge mouth open. Clamped down, tore with my teeth, tossed my head.

<Aaaaahhhh!> something cried in my head. <Who's biting me? Geez, a chunk of my tail is gone! Hey, I was using that!>

That voice — it sounded familiar. Jake. Jake! I'd attacked him!

Suddenly, I remembered who I was. Rachel.

I struggled against the shark brain. Fought to regain control. Tobias had warned us. Stupidly, arrogantly, I'd thought he was being overly cautious.

I'd been wrong.

<Jake, are you OK?> I asked. <I — I lost control.>

<Yeah, I'm OK. I'm having a hard time calming the shark's mind, too,> Jake said. <The blood is driving it crazy.>

<Cassie? Tobias? Ax? You guys in the driver's seat?>

<I'm cool,> Tobias said.

<I am in control.> Ax.

<We need to focus on something else,> Cassie said tensely. <Keep our own, human minds alert.>

We swam on. First Jake. Then Cassie, Ax, Tobias and me. Concentrating on the goal — stop the Helmacrons — to avoid eating one another alive.

The current dragged us along the narrow tunnel of blood. A tunnel not completely dark, but extremely dim.

Globs of stuff floated along next to us. Brushed off the tunnel walls, bounced off our shark bodies. Some were rod-shaped and about the size of grapefruit. Others, just shapeless pieces of material. Still others, fuzzy balls, like Ping-Pong balls stuck all over with cotton.

<What's wrong with Marco's blood?> I asked. <It's not red.>

<You're seeing plasma,> Cassie explained. <Blood only looks red because it contains so many red blood cells.>

<Oh.>

<Hey, check it out,> Cassie said. <Those are red blood cells! The dark red ones pressing up against our gills. About the size of a serving platter. Somehow we're capturing the oxygen molecules without sucking in the blood cells.>

I'm not much of a sightseer. Generally, sightseeing puts me in a tedium-induced rage.

This was different.

I was happy to be a tourist, especially if it would keep me from going cannibal. Besides, how many suburban girls get to travel down a human vein as a tiny hammerhead shark?

Disney has nothing on the Animorphs.

Red blood cell. Red blood cell. Red blood cell. After I'd seen a few thousand, I stopped paying attention to them and started to focus on the other floating shapes.

<What was that?> I demanded.

Something seriously small passed in front of my eyes. To the sub-mini shark, it was about the size and shape of a pill. A pill with little spikes covering it. A 3-D millipede.

<What?> Cassie asked eagerly.

The thing looked out of place. Sharp and

pointed in a world where everything else was soft and oval.

<Something strange.>

<All sorts of stuff travels in the blood,> Cassie said. <Food particles. Waste. Hormones.>

<Hormones?> Jake interrupted. <We're swimming in hormones?>

Again, I spotted the spiny thing. It wasn't just bumping along in the current. It seemed to have a purpose. A mind or a will. I watched as it brushed up against a red blood cell, probed it, then bounced away.

I'm not big on superstition or New Age crap. Don't read my horoscope. Never had my fortune told. But I had a feeling about that spiky thing. Some primitive, instinctual part of my human brain didn't like it.

<Rachel?> Tobias called. <Come on. You're falling behind.>

I powered my tail and caught up.

<There's a branch up ahead,> Jake said.

<Listen!> Cassie. <I think I can hear the Helmacrons.>

<So they aren't dead,> Jake said grimly.

<Arrrrrggghhhh!> The pill from hell! It was on my morph. Probing me!

<Get it off!> I yelled.

<What?> Tobias asked.

<Pay attention! Small spiky vitamin pills. I think they could be dangerous!>

<I see one,> Ax said. <Now it is gone.>

<What happened?>

<A large translucent blob surrounded and consumed it,> Ax explained.

<I saw it, too,> Jake said. <The blob ate it like Pac Man.>

Silence.

Then Cassie began to laugh.

<What's so funny?> I said shakily.

<This is amazing,> Cassie said. <Ax and Jake just saw Marco's immune system fight off an invader. That Pac Man was a white blood cell.>

<So, the spiky thing?> I asked.

<A bacterium or a virus,> Cassie said.

<What kind?>

<How should I know?> Cassie replied. <The important thing is that Marco's immune system is working.>

Oh, yeah. That's the important thing.

Chapter 18

We continued down the tunnel that was Marco's vein. When we reached the branch Jake had pointed out, we followed the bloodstream into a wider tunnel.

The Helmacrons' voices were growing slightly louder.

Then, suddenly—

Dead end!

The vein just . . . stopped.

We had stumbled into a fun house. Tunnels opened all around us, in every direction. Above the shark's head, below its belly. Each one seemed to be a different size and shape. Some big enough for us to pass through. Some far too small.

The current had also stopped. I turned the

hammerhead to the right and swam in a small circle. Hovering without progressing.

<Any idea which way we should go?> Jake asked.

<I'm thinking,> Cassie said.

The blood cells and miscellaneous blobs that had been washing along beside us were still with us, but no more joined them.

<Where does human blood travel after it leaves the stomach?> Ax asked calmly, almost conversationally.

<That's what I'm trying to remember!> Cassie answered.

<Are not these basic facts about your own physiology taught in human schools?> Ax said. <On the Andalite home world, the youngest child is able to—>

<Ax. Would you please shut up?> I said.

Bump.

Tobias, knocking up against me. <And spread out, you guys!>

<Touchy, touchy.>

<Don't you feel it?> Tobias asked. <The . . . uneasiness.>

I bumped into Jake. Turned to the right, swam in another tight circle.

<The hammerhead mind is uneasy,> Ax agreed.

The shark sensed danger. Not fear. Sharks have no understanding of fear. The shark was calm, confident. But it sensed some sort of change in the liquid surrounding us and it wanted to get out.

Maybe this is how sharks feel swimming in polluted ocean waters. I don't know. The shark's mind didn't offer any explanation. It just said: *get out. Now.*

I clamped down on the shark's mind. Now wasn't the time to panic.

<Acid?> Ax asked.

I tuned into the shark's skin. But there was no pain. Just a dim sort of tingle that wasn't unpleasant. Nothing like the all-out agony of being in the stomach's violent digestive juices.

<I don't think we—>

<Look,> Tobias interrupted. <The globs.>

One right in front of me. It wasn't any particular shape or colour. A fat molecule? A tiny bit of adrenaline? No way of knowing. And then. . .

<It exploded!> I exclaimed.

As if a bomb had gone off inside, the glob silently broke into a thousand pieces.

<Watch one of the rod-shaped things,> Cassie said.

I twisted my hammerhead and turned in another tight, right-hand circle. Noted a rod-shaped thing a few centimetres off to my right. And then, suddenly, it was round and slightly green.

<Presto chango,> Jake said.

<Something is transforming the cellular structure of the molecules around us,> Ax said.

<I think we're in some kind of sorting device. Look. The round blobs go into that tunnel, there. But the rod-shaped ones go up there.>

Weird, but true. Some of the molecules were lining up for the girls' toilet; others, for the boys'.

I bumped up against Ax. <Sorry,> I muttered. Turned to the right to swim out of his way.

To the right.

Again.

<OK,> I said. <I am seriously drawn to a particular tunnel.>

<Yeah, me, too,> said Tobias.

<The shark is definitely compelled.> Ax.

<It's like Rachel at a fifty-per-cent-off sale at The Gap,> Cassie said. <Resistance is futile. Oh. I think I know where we are.>

<And that would be—>

<In the liver.>

<What is a liver?> Ax asked.

<An organ. The part of the human body that filters out impurities,> Cassie explained. <Assuming the liver thinks we're impurities — and it must — it's pushing us into the colon.>

Suddenly, the current felt stronger. Maybe I was just more aware of it. <The colon? You mean, we're going to be waste?>

<Product,> Cassie confirmed.

<Thanks a lot, Marco.>

<If we are expelled, we will not reach the heart.> Ax, calmly stating the obvious as only Ax can.

<We've got to swim,> Jake said.

<Fine,> I agreed. <But which way?>

<Towards the heart,> Cassie said.

<Which is—?> I asked.

<Above the liver,> Cassie said.

<Who said you were directionally challenged?>

About a dozen tunnels went up to the left and up to the right. One tunnel seemed to go straight up.

<Eenie, meenie, minie, moe?> Ax said.

<You really have been on Earth too long,> I told him. <You'll never fit in on the Andalite home world now.>

<I would miss Saturday-morning cartoons,> Ax said.

Thump, *thump*.

And then. . .

Click! My brain made one of those sudden leaps. Like two puzzle pieces falling together. <Marco's heart!>

Thump, *thump*.

Thump, *thump*.

Louder. Coming from all directions at once.

<Can we follow the sound?>

<I can't tell exactly where it's coming from,> Jake said.

<Think,> Cassie said. <What would the liver send to the heart?>

<Blood,> I said.

<Great. Follow that red blood cell!>

Chapter 19

Marco

When I finally got home from my pathetic attempt at breaking and entering, I put on a long-sleeved sweatshirt. Couldn't let Dad see my wrist. Didn't want him to know I'd been trying to rob some kid when his deranged dog took a chunk out of me.

I dabbed some antiseptic on the puncture marks. Added a little antibiotic cream. Wished for ibuprofen. My whole arm throbbed.

But so what?

A little dog bite wasn't going to kill me. The Helmacrons had that under control.

In a way, I welcomed the pain. It reminded me I was alive. For now.

The afternoon dragged on.

And I had no idea what was going on inside me.

Hours passed and all I heard from my friends were occasional strange orders.

Don't sneeze.

Don't eat or drink anything.

I wanted to tell them to include me in their thought-speak. Maybe. I mean, did I really want to know what a group of morphing warriors and egomaniacal lunatics were doing to my delicate internal tissues?

I contacted Mr King. Had the Chee show up for dinner as Jake, Rachel and Cassie.

Dinner.

I told my dad I was sick.

Just after the sun went down, I fell asleep, sprawled across my bed. About an hour later I woke up feeling weird. Sweaty. Wild. Angry.

Angry . . . at the Helmacrons! It wasn't fair that I couldn't protect myself. Stupid freakin'. . .

The usual hang around and chill out routine was not going to happen. I was way too restless. Needed to do something. Got up and started to pace. Door to windows. Windows to door. Back. Forth.

And the anger continued to grow. Welled and surged and wouldn't be held in check by my usual habit of black humour, transforming tragedy into comedy. There wasn't one joke in me.

Maybe I just missed my audience.

Anyway, I was in an exceptionally foul mood.

A soft knock at the door. It opened. My dad stuck his head in. "Marco, hey, I thought I heard you moving around. How are you feeling?"

"Um, fine."

Dad pursed his lips. Came in and put a hand against my cheek. "You're flushed. And you feel a bit hot."

I turned away. "I said I was fine!"

"OK, OK." He was taken aback by my reaction. "Well, if you're feeling better . . . Nora and I have that dinner party. It's a work thing. If you don't need me to stay with you."

I immediately saw the opportunity. "Go," I said soothingly. "I'm just going to rest. Read that book for English."

He probably didn't buy that last part, but he headed for the door.

"OK," he said. "Well, I'll leave the number on the refrigerator. Give us a call if you start to feel worse."

"I'll be fine," I said again, through suddenly clenched teeth.

Dad left.

Ten minutes later I heard the car pull out of the driveway.

I waited another couple of minutes. Then I went down to the basement. Rooted around in the freezer until I found a steak. Upstairs in the kitchen, nuked it in the microwave until it was

defrosted and warm. Then I got my bike out of the garage.

I was going to get the camera.

So what if I couldn't morph? So what if my friends couldn't help me? So what if Cujo had practically ripped my arm off?

That camera was mine.

The ratty-looking Chee was still on guard. That meant that the camera, if not the kid, was still inside.

For about half a second I wondered if I should ask for his help. Maybe he could throw a holo around me, make it easier to sneak into the apartment.

Rejected the idea. It would probably violate the Chee's code of non-violence. What a joke.

I could do this alone.

The kid's apartment building looked even more decrepit at night. But I felt no fear. I walked straight over the fence and across the concrete lot to the fire escape. It was still hanging down the way I'd left it. I charged up.

Cujo was waiting.

"Rrrrrrr!" He growled deep in his throat when he saw me on the fire escape.

Then he flung himself madly against the window. Totally airborne. Toenails clicking on the wooden sill. Drool flying. Teeth gleaming.

I grabbed the bottom of the rickety window and yanked it up about halfway.

"ArfARFARFARFARFARF!" Cujo's snapping jaws were centimetres from my throat.

"Stuff it," I said, tossing the steak into the room.

He lay down with it between his paws. Licked. Slobbered. Seemed to be having a hard time eating it. Something was wrong with his jaw. Maybe he'd lost a tooth gnawing my arm off.

I heaved the window open further. Dropped down on to the floor and eased around the slavering dog. The camera was a few metres away, still sitting on the kid's desk.

I'd just closed my fingers on the bright yellow box when I heard voices in the hallway, surprisingly close.

Cujo heard them, too. He rose to his feet and growled at me. Blocking my only exit.

Door. People. Cops. Juvenile detention.

Window. Cujo.

Two options.

Both bad.

Either way, I was going to get caught.

Chapter 20

Rachel

Thump, *thump.*

Pause.

Thump, *thump.*

As we swam the beating grew louder and louder, until it was impossible to hear anything else. Impossible to know if the Helmacrons were near.

Ax didn't ask questions. Tobias didn't make any dark observations. Jake didn't talk strategy. Cassie didn't point out landmarks.

We were overwhelmed by the incredible reverberating noise surrounding us. The sound of Marco's heart beating.

THUMP! *THUMP!*

Pause.

THUMP! *THUMP!*

Each beat vibrated through my body, overpowering any human thought or emotion. We didn't have a plan for capturing the Helmacrons. I didn't try to think of one.

Closer. Closer. Thump, *thump*. The sound became so intense I felt like it would blow me apart. But it was a wonderful sound. As long as we experienced that thump, *thump* Marco was still alive.

The red blood cells we were chasing had changed colour. They were darker now, maroon, the colour of a scab. Cassie didn't need to explain what was happening. I'd read the *Magic School Bus*, too.

Close to the heart, the level of oxygen in the blood cells was low. The cells would pass through the heart and then into the lungs to pick up more oxygen.

Less oxygen in the blood cells meant less oxygen for the sharks. But we couldn't turn back. We had to stop the Helmacrons from killing Marco. Do or die.

The vein through which we were travelling grew larger. Other veins emptied into it and the current picked up. This time, it was like moving from a small street to a larger road to a busy dual carriageway. And finally, to a six-lane motorway.

Ahead was a sort of aperture of flesh. As the current swept us along, it opened wider and

wider. Fluttering in front of the opening were three red sheets of flesh. They moved like curtains blowing in an open window. Like those felt strips at the beginning of a car wash. As the valve widened, they blew inside.

The current was smooth but powerful. The heart was sucking us in.

Closer. . .

Closer. . .

Closer! Then—

SLLLUMP!

The aperture closed. The curtains of flesh sealed together with a wet, sucking noise.

We slowed, stopped. We were in a vast opening just outside the heart, surrounded by an ocean of blood.

<That's OK!> Cassie said. <That valve must be to keep the blood from flowing back this direction.>

THUMP!

<How are we going to stay inside the heart? How are we going to stop ourselves from being swept out into the lungs?> Tobias called. <I'm not sure we can fight this current!>

<We don't know if the Helmacrons can, either. Just be ready to fight!> Jake shouted. <Assuming the Helmacrons are inside the heart now!>

THUMP!

The valve began to open. The curtains began to billow in.

Then — we flowed into the first chamber of the heart.

Things happened fast.

<Turn around!> I shouted. <Swim against the current!>

Furious turbulence! Blood was flowing past so fast I could hardly suck in any oxygen. Imagine swimming up Niagara Falls. And the walls were contracting like a rubbish compactor!

<Obey me, foolish male! Dracon beams will only fire in liquid if you increase the power to full!>

<I grow weary of your meddling, female! I will blast on low if I choose!>

<The Helmacrons!> Tobias shouted.

<Where are they?> Cassie yelled.

<Jake, they can't shoot!> I hissed.

<Stop!> Jake cried in general thought-speak. <Put down your weapons and we will help you out of here. We will even let you use the power source.>

<Hah-HAH!> one of the Helmacrons shouted. <Too late! We shoot on my count! One!>

I couldn't see the Helmacrons. But I could smell them. Somewhere in the heart. Five of them. Maybe tangled in one of the tissue sprays that connected the walls like chaotic gothic arches. Maybe bobbing in the thrashing ocean of blood.

I didn't know.

I didn't care.

And I didn't care what had happened to the other four Helmacrons. Maybe the liver had taken them. Maybe they had been washed away by the last heartbeat.

The Helmacrons were enormous compared to my shark morph.

And armed. But I was going to stop them from shooting if it was the last thing I did.

All of these thoughts passed in about one second.

I turned my flattened rudder of a head and began to swim. The excellent shark sense of smell told me one of the Helmacrons was to my left.

<Prince Jake, we have to stop them now!>

<Go!> Jake shouted. <Now!>

Powering through a forest of tissue strands, an ocean of blood. Hunting for the Helmacrons!

Tissue!

Turn — left!

<Two!> the Helmacron shouted.

No!

Frantically I fought the current. Pushed and strained with my tail, my flippers. Struggled for every paltry centimetre.

And meanwhile, the walls around me closed in as Marco's heart prepared to beat.

Tissue!

Turn — another left!

Push, push, push!

The shark was exhausted. And the Helmacron smell was only the faintest bit stronger.

THUMP!

The first part of Marco's heartbeat.

The heartbeat that might be his last.

Chapter 21

Marco

"What's wrong with Buster?" A voice, just outside the door. Female. Maybe the photographer's mother, sister, aunt.

Buster?

Oh, come on. This dog was no Buster.

Bruiser, maybe. Fang, Killer, Psycho. But not Buster.

Buster's bloodshot eyes were on me. Blocking the window. My only escape.

I could hide under the bed. Except the metal frame was only about ten centimetres off the ground. No way.

The door handle turned.

I jumped for the wardrobe and crashed into the flimsy sliding doors. Great. The woman in the hall had to hear that. Too late to run. What the heck had I been thinking!

I closed the doors behind me, scooted down on to a pile of sweaty-smelling clothes, backed towards the corner.

"ARFARFARFARFARF!"

Whooosh! Buster's head was a wedge, shoving open one of the sliding doors. He bounded into the wardrobe and went for my ankle.

"Rrrrooo — ARFARFARFARFARF!"

A strange rage filled me. I lifted the shoe.

A very low voice in my head said: *dangerous dog. Be afraid.*

No.

"Buster! Good dog!"

Buster turned towards the sound of his master. A split-second hesitation before biting off my head. That gave me just long enough to decide.

Morph — or get caught.

Morph — or get chewed up like a dog biscuit.

Yeah, I'd promised Jake I wouldn't morph. But I hadn't heard from my so-called friends in hours and hours. For all I knew they could be dead.

A little voice in my head, that intangible but incredibly annoying thing called a conscience, was concerned. *Marco*, it said, *can't you see something is wrong with you? With what you're doing? Where's your compassion? It's just a dumb dog, doing what he's supposed to do. And your friends, their lives are valuable.*

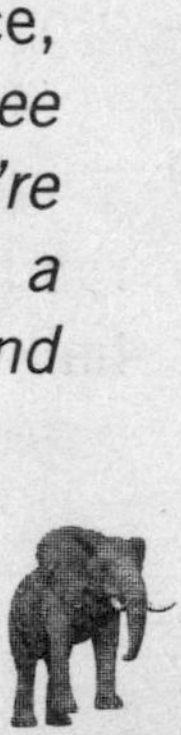

Roach, I answered.

I felt the changes begin at the same time I heard footsteps crossing the room.

Each morph is different. I'd gone roach plenty of times before. But each experience is completely unique.

This time, my skin hardened first.

Then, vision pixilated. Compound roach eyes, with about two thousand lenses, ballooned up out of my eye sockets.

Two thousand Busters.

Two thousand sets of snapping teeth.

Four legs exploded out of my sides and I fell forwards. My arms fused to my sides, then re-emerged as delicate wings.

Buster tilted his head and moaned as I shrank down to the size of a 10p piece.

Don't eat me, I warned him silently. *I have enough problems already*.

My antennae twitched as the roach's amazing sense of smell surged to life. Roaches can smell anything. The wardrobe smelled of sweat and dog pee and washing powder.

Buster took a step back and moaned again.

The wardrobe door burst open.

"Oh — sick!" someone yelled. "I'm going to sue that filthy landlord! Honey, bring a shoe! I just caught the world's biggest roach!"

Then came the change I had been waiting for.

With a sickening lurch, my innards began to twist and change.

<Aaaaahhhhhhh!> someone yelled in my head.

<Marco is morphing!> Cassie shouted. <Something must be wrong! Marco must be in trouble!>

Ah, so now I could hear them all. Must be in morph.

<We do not know how this will affect us,> Ax said unnecessarily. <It could be deadly.>

<Marco, cut it out, now!> Rachel screamed.

<That's an order!> Jake shouted.

My friends were still alive.

And they sounded terrified.

Good for them.

Chapter 22

Rachel

A centimetre.

One more centimetre and a Helmacron would be down to three legs. I pumped my tail hard. Opened my mouth to bite. Then—

THUMP!

I was yanked away from the Helmacron. Spun, head over tail. Another aperture — this one on the opposite side of the chamber — rapidly opened. It grew from a crack, to a hole, to a chasm.

Blood started to flow out of the chamber, sweeping all of us along with it.

<Are the Helmacrons being washed out, too?> Jake shouted.

<I can't tell!> I answered.

<Try to stay inside!>

I strained. Tried with every cell to resist the sucking of the current. And still I lost ground.

<I am unable to maintain my position!> Ax called.

And then—

The chamber all around me began to shift and blur! The forest of tissue melted like heated wax.

But the changes continued. The chamber surrounding us shrank down, down, down. Half the size it was. Half that. Then half that. Smaller, smaller, smaller.

The root-like tissues came unglued. Bounced like loose electrical cables, and then sucked up into the walls.

<Fiendish alien! You will not destroy the Helmacron knights! We will ru — agggghhh!>

SLOOONG!

The walls separating this chamber of the heart from the next stretched like a rubber band and exploded. The red blood faded to rose, then pink, then white.

Air! Would we still have air without the red blood cells? I gasped and found I could still breathe.

The noise was deafening. I wanted to cover my ears, but I had no ears, no hands.

An earthquake, a tornado, a volcano, a tidal wave, a monsoon!

SLLLURPPPP!

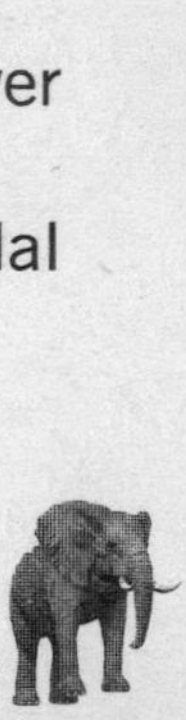

<You will grovel for this!>

<Marco,> Jake shouted, <you'd better be in serious trouble! Because things are not pretty in here!>

Bong! Bong! Bong! Bong!

<Ahhhhhh!> I screamed. An enormous nightmare glob of pulsing organ bulged out in front of me. Then it did a fast-forward shrivel and disappeared.

<Watch out!> Tobias shouted.

What looked like a femur poked into the chamber and caught me on the head. I spun, knocking into Jake and one of the Helmacrons.

<Just relax,> Cassie urged. <It should be over soon!>

Seconds later—

Poof! The hurricane was over. Marco's morph was complete.

<Hey, you guys?> Marco called with a laugh. <Still alive or what?>

<Still alive,> Jake said shakily.

We were squashed together in a tiny space filled with bluish-white liquid. The walls surrounding us were smooth — and they were squeezing together. Another rubbish compactor, only doll's-house-sized.

<Probably an insect of some sort. Marco, what kind of morph are we in?> Ax said.

<Isn't it obvious?> Marco said nastily.

<Just tell us,> Tobias replied.

<You haven't told me anything for hours! Now I'm supposed to be Mr Communication?>

<Oh, very mature,> I snapped.

OK, so Marco had good reason to feel the way he did. Five of his friends up his nose, Dracon beams blasting his stomach lining, etc, etc, etc. But, come on. He sounded like a spoiled two year old.

Marco was often annoying but never stupid.

<Would you like to explain why you morphed?> Jake demanded. <Why you morphed when I told you it could kill us?>

<I plead the fifth.>

Jake, to us. <If I were a real general, I'd court-martial his sorry. . .>

Then, from a jumble of alien parts, a Helmacron shouted. <Hah-HAH! No doubt you thought we were killed by the transforming of our pitiful hostage. But we are still alive! We shall rule the universe yet!>

And before any of us — Jake or Cassie, Ax or Tobias, before even I — could do anything to stop them. . .

The Helmacrons fired in unison.

Tseeew!

Tseeew!

Tseeew!

Tseeew!

Tseeew!

<No!> I screamed.

And then . . . silence.

<Marco!> Cassie cried. <Marco, can you hear us?>

Nothing.

<Marco!>

<Marco!> Cassie cried again. A wrenching sound, horrified, full of pain.

<He can't answer you, Cassie,> Jake said, his voice strangely flat.

Next I heard Tobias's voice. <Who would have predicted this? Who would have thought the Helmacrons were more dangerous than the Yeerks?>

"Neep! Neep! Neep!" A cheer went up from the Helmacrons.

A strange coldness swept through me. Not sadness. Not exactly. In a way, I was prepared for this. We had been through so many missions, so much danger. That one of us should die seemed . . . inevitable. Unavoidable.

And then—

Fury.

A wave of fury like a kick to the gut.

I wanted those Helmacrons dead.

Chapter 23

O Majestic Leader, Humans are a race of fools! We told them time and time again that Helmacrons do not surrender! And yet they delude themselves, believing that we would deal with them simply because we have suffered minor injury! Does it not make you laugh, and prove that we are the only fit rulers of the universe?

— From the log of the Helmacron Females

"Neep! Neep! Ne — Agggghhhh!"

I attacked while the Helmacrons were still cheering Marco's death. I bit clear though a Helmacron's leg with my powerful shark jaw.

The Helmacron jerked. He didn't lose his balance, but I felt something heavy fall near me.

<Cassie, Ax, grab the Dracon beam!> I shouted. <Jake, Tobias, hack through the walls.>

<But Marco—> Tobias said.

<Marco is dead!> I said savagely. <Do it!>

<No!> Jake shouted.

<We have to,> Cassie said quietly.

<We must fight to save ourselves,> Ax said. <There will be time for mourning later.>

<Fine,> Jake said bitterly.

<The treacherous aliens have severed my limb!> the Helmacron cried. <But I shall still hobble on to victory!>

<We must seize the power source!> another Helmacron shouted. <The brave Helmacron females shall lead the way!>

<We got the beam!> Cassie shouted. <Now what?>

<We'll tunnel through to the lungs,> I said. <You and Ax get inside, demorph, and turn that beam on them. The rest of us will bite a few holes in these creeps.>

<One problem,> Cassie said. <That Dracon beam is bigger than the human me. How am I going to pick it up?>

<Ant power,> I said.

<Schwarzenegger, right.>

Whoooosssh!

A pillow of air escaped from Marco's lung.

<Bingo!> Jake yelled.

<We got the lungs!> Tobias shouted.

By then, the other four Helmacrons had lost a limb. Been forced to drop their weapons. Quieted down a bit. And when they realized we were now armed — well, they were suddenly interested in dealing.

<Perhaps a strategic alliance is in order,> one of the Helmacron males said. <You will help us power up our ship.>

<And you will?> Jake prompted.

<Conquer all of the other planets in the universe before returning to crush Earth!>

<Tempting,> Jake said.

<Don't deal with these idiots,> I said angrily. <I say we waste them and bail.>

<I've had enough death for one day,> Cassie said. <Letting them power up their ship won't do any harm. If we'd suggested that in the beginning, Marco might still be alive.>

<OK, Helmacrons, you have two choices,> Jake said. <Choice one: we march out of here together. You unshrink us. We let you use the blue box once to power up your engines and get off our planet.>

<Never! Helmacrons are the masters of the—>

<Shut up and listen to your second choice!> I shouted.

<We are listening to your unworthy scheme!>

<Choice two,> Jake said coldly. <Die.>

<You killed our friend,> I added. <And let me tell you, payback is no fun.>

The Helmacrons blustered and complained. But they agreed to surrender and unshrink us. They didn't really have a choice.

In the lungs we demorphed. Tobias to hawk. Ax to Andalite. The rest of us to human.

And then, we marched out of the body. Out through what Cassie later called spiracles, or the breathing holes on either side of a cockroach's body. We kept the Helmacrons under guard like prisoners of war. We moved fast, anxious to abandon the corpse. A corpse that was all that was left of Marco.

Zombie-like, I walked. Looked straight ahead. Didn't talk. Too busy processing.

Marco, my fellow warrior and, yeah, even friend . . . gone for ever. Killed. Not by the Yeerks, as we all half-expected to be, but by a race of tiny egomaniacs.

There was no justice, poetic or otherwise, in that.

Chapter 24

"This isn't the barn," Cassie said.

Wherever we were, it was dark and vast. At least it seemed that way. Then again, we weren't much bigger than bacteria.

"Does anyone see the Helmacron ship?" Jake asked.

<No,> Tobias said.

<If we cannot find the ship we will not be able to return to our full size,> Ax said.

"Duh."

"Ax, just guard the Helmacrons," Jake said.

<Yes, Prince Jake.> Ax held a Dracon beam on our little band of gimpy, marble-eyed prisoners. His tail hovered above his head, ready to strike.

"Tobias?" Jake said.

<I'll try to figure out where we are,> Tobias

said wearily. With difficulty, he gained some altitude and was lost in the darkness.

Jake shook his head. "Somehow I imagined we'd come out in the barn and the Helmacron ship would just be there."

"Where did Marco go? He was supposed to stay put," I complained. Then felt bad for complaining.

<The ship may have been destroyed,> Ax said.

"Now there's a happy thought."

Cassie laughed grimly. "I wonder how long it will be before humans invent an anti-shrinking ray."

<A long, long time,> Ax stated.

"Look on the bright side," I said, manically. Desperately. "We're useless to the Yeerks. We're much too small to be Controllers now."

"Useless to humans, too," Jake snapped. "We can't fight Visser Three when we're the size of a shredded fingernail clipping."

"Don't worry about the fight," I said. "We're going to spend the rest of our lives just trying to get home."

Tobias was back. <I didn't see the ship,> he reported. <But I think we may be in Marco's wardrobe. I think that big cliff over there is a hiking boot.>

"What is he?" Jake asked, glancing over his shoulder to the dark, looming mass that had once been our friend.

<Roach, I think.>

"ARFARFARFARFARFARF!" A vicious-sounding dog, somewhere nearby.

<We can hear a dog barking,> Ax said. <It is likely a dog's voice has a different frequency than that of a human.>

"That doesn't sound like Euclid," Cassie said musingly.

"Roach," Jake said bitterly. "It's Marco's last joke. Roaches are, like, impossible to kill. Pretty ironic, huh?"

"I think we should organize a search party," I said. "I'll go eagle. Tobias and I can try to determine if we really are in Marco's house."

"Jake's right," Cassie said suddenly. "I did an oral report on roaches in year six. Nothing kills them. Cutting off their heads doesn't kill them. Submerging them in water doesn't kill them—"

"Enough with the Animal Planet report," I said. "We're a fraction of a centimetre high and probably kilometres from home. It's time to focus."

"I'm not just babbling," Cassie argued. "Listen. I'm saying: nothing kills a roach. Not even stopping its heart. They have some sort of back-up system."

"You think we can still reach him?" Jake demanded.

"It's possible."

This was too good to believe. A tiny breath of hope against the cold wall of death.

Naturally, I was suspicious. “Hasn’t he been in that morph for more than two hours?”

“Ax-man?” Jake asked.

<One hour, fifty-five minutes,> Ax said, moving his stalk eyes towards us and keeping his main eyes on the strangely silent prisoners.

“Five minutes,” Cassie said. “There’s hope.”

I looked up, up, up. On one side — an enormous leg spiked with disgusting, dirty hairs. On the other — a shiny smooth nut-case wall of armour.

The roach was giving off a dusky, filthy smell. A roach smell. But at that moment, the highly evolved roach body looked beautiful to me. Marco had ultimately picked the perfect morph.

And he just might be alive to gloat about it.

We started to yell.

“Marco — morph out!” Jake cried desperately.

“Come on, Marco!” Cassie shouted.

<You have only five Earth minutes left!> Ax yelled.

<Morph out!>

“Do it now!”

No response.

<He’s not moving,> Tobias said.

“Maybe he’s in a coma,” Cassie said.

“Or sleeping,” Jake added, attempting a joke. Bad attempt.

"Marco," Cassie said. "Come on, now. Listen to me. If you're in there, start to demorph. I'll help you through."

<C'mon buddy, don't get stuck as a roach,> Tobias said desperately.

"Dude," I said. "How dumb is it to live the rest of your life in a body that makes girls scream in terror? Your dating life is so over, before it's even begun."

<Four minutes,> Ax said.

"Marco, man, come on," Jake pleaded. "We need you."

"Yeah, we haven't had a good laugh all day."

Who knows what finally reached him? Cassie's gentle coaching? Tobias's too-real fear? Jake's pleading? My pathetic jokes? Maybe even Ax's cold countdown? I'm not even sure any of our puny voices, thought-speak or not, got through.

All I know is that the hairy leg near me began to puff outwards. Growing, growing — until it was a roach-coloured wall. We ran to keep from getting squashed.

<We have been viciously tricked!> a Helmacron shouted. <The transforming alien is not really dead!>

Ax pointed the Dracon beam. <Shut. Up,> he said calmly.

The Helmacrons' marble eyes all turned to face Marco.

Then—

A rumbling of sound.

<I believe Marco is awake,> Ax informed us.

"Marco. Man! You are in serious doo-doo." Jake tried to sound serious, but he didn't.

"Ax, he probably can't hear my voice, so ask him where we are!" I said. Then I smacked Marco on his growing human arm. Ridiculous. All less than a centimetre of me.

<Marco, Rachel has just hit you in anger. And Jake demands to know why you morphed when he expressly forbade you to do so. However, at the moment there is no need to answer this question as I will be unable to hear your response.>

"ARFARFARFARFARFARF!" Cujo, in the hallway.

Then, a rumbling of sound. A massive human voice.

There was no way I could hear or understand Marco's words, but I bet he said something like this: "Oh, man. I'm getting it from both sides! Everybody's always blaming me! This whole thing is Rachel's fault. If she hadn't hit me in the first place, I wouldn't have fallen and hit my head. . ."

"Ax, tell Marco to stop whining and thank us for saving him from a life under the kitchen sink!"

Ax did. Here's what I know Marco said: "Remind me to send flowers after I save your sorry butts."

Chapter 25

Marco morphed a gull.

We clung to him. The five of us, and our five prisoners.

<Prince Jake instructs that you not forget the camera.>

Marco explained to us where we were as he bird-walked out of the wardrobe, hopped up on to the desk and grabbed the camera with his beak. Then, we flew through the open window and headed towards Cassie's barn.

Now that he was in morph, Marco could engage in two-way communication with Ax and Tobias.

<That crappy dog attacked me!> he told us as we passed into the dusky light. <Practically chewed my hand off.>

"How'd you get away?" Cassie asked, via Ax.

<Even though I was dripping copious amounts of blood, I performed like a brave and stalwart knight and marched down the ladder of rattling steel!> Marco said. <Then I rode home on my trusty purple steed.>

"Please tell me you're not going to be imitating the Helmacrons for the next two months," Jake said.

<Nah,> Marco said. <I'm going to be too busy conquering the universe.>

Had we actually missed this guy? Hard to believe.

<Dog bites can be nasty,> Cassie said. <Did you have a doctor look at it?>

<Please, like I had the time? Besides, when I morphed and demorphed, the thing was gone. I'm perfect again.>

"Yeah, and we'll talk later about your brilliant decision to disobey orders." Jake. "I just know you had a good reason."

<Uh . . . yeah, I hope so.>

"I wonder what's on that film," I said.

Jake frowned. "We'll never know. Developing it is too risky. We'll burn it as soon as we get to the barn."

We did.

Marco had hidden the Helmacron ship in the freezer, along with the blue box. Ax hooked everything up and forced the protesting Helmacrons to unshrink us.

Relief.

Then we let them power up their ship and take off.

"Promise us you'll never come back to Earth," Jake said as the Helmacrons hovered in front of the barn door.

<You have our word, as honourable female servants of the Helmacron empire!>

<A Helmacron male would never lie!>

At the same time, I noticed the blue box beginning to elevate. I couldn't see the Helmacrons minuscule tractor beam, but I knew it was there.

Marco and I both jumped to grab the box. I snagged it. We even managed not to hit our heads together.

Cassie stowed the blue box somewhere safe. Again, for security, she didn't tell us where. Then we all headed home for a little quality time with our parents. I had piles of homework. I was researching the Salem witch-hunts on the Internet when I flashed on that strange spiky thing we saw in Marco's bloodstream.

Ten minutes later I found it on the website from the Centre for Disease Control.

A sketchy line drawing of the spiky thing.

A rabies virus.

The dog bite Marco had told us about. . .

What I read about rabies didn't make me feel all warm and fuzzy inside.

Rabies is not a pretty disease. Get it and you have two choices: start a series of injections within three days. Or die. Die after going awfully, violently insane.

Bottom line: if Marco hadn't morphed, to roach or anything else, he'd be dying. He wouldn't have known he had rabies so he wouldn't have started the treatment in time. When he'd morphed in the kid's wardrobe, almost twelve hours had already gone by.

Other bottom line: it was clear to me that Marco had morphed not to upset Jake or to save his own skinny butt. Not to betray us or because he valued his own life over ours.

He'd morphed because the disease had already begun to twist his mind and distort his judgment. He'd morphed against direct orders because he was slowly going insane.

This was good news. Marco wasn't dying and with this interesting piece of information I could get him off the hook with Jake and the others.

I reached for the phone. Stopped.

Smirked. Maybe in the morning.

Don't miss

ANIMORPHS®

43 The Test

No one said anything. Silent agreement.

Except for Cassie.

Her eyes got wide. She began to stand up.

"None of you guys are really thinking about this," she said in a voice that made a couple of older kids sitting at the table next to ours look up.

"Shhh."

"No," she said. "It's wrong. I won't. I don't want to judge you guys, but you're talking about strategy and risk like this is some computer game. Like there aren't others involved. Have you forgotten that we're supposed to be in this to save lives?"

Jake put his hand on her shoulder and gently encouraged her to sit back down. No one seemed to know what to say. She continued. She spoke very quietly, but urgently.

"Has anyone stopped to think that we'll be responsible for the death of hundreds, maybe thousands of people? People who already suffer the worst fate imaginable? And not that any of you care, but we'll be killing thousands of defenceless Yeerks right along with them."

"My God, you mean we'd be killing Yeerks?" Marco said with a straight face. "That's . . . that's unthinkable!"

No one laughed.

"Let her finish," Rachel whispered.

"They're not all like Visser Three," Cassie went on. "We know that. Some of the Yeerks and Controllers are just kids like us. They never had a choice. They participate or they're eliminated. And it's not like they get the information they need to make an informed decision. If you'd been raised since birth on empire propaganda, you'd fight to take over Earth, too."

"You make an interesting argument," Ax said through a mouthful of nachos. "But there are a lot of inconsistencies between what you say and what you do." He swallowed noisily. "How can you make this argument knowing what you've done in the past?"

"That's different," Cassie responded forcefully. "I'm not against defending myself and you guys. I hate violence, but self-defence is justified, in all societies. Unlike murdering people. . ."

"Killing slugs," Marco corrected.

"Killing Yeerks when they're defenceless, when they're not engaged in battle, when they're not actively threatening our lives . . . no! You don't . . . why can't you . . . can't you see!" She stopped. I could almost feel the passion radiating from her body. "It's . . . it's just not right."

"But they are threatening our lives," Rachel insisted. "Not just ours, everyone's. Just by being who they are."

"Yeah, and why do you think they're at the Yeerk pool?" Marco put in. "I can tell you this much. It's not because they're planning Earth Day activities."

"Look, during World War Two we bombed factories and roads and railways. Even ordinary cities. Just because someone's not wearing a uniform or carrying a weapon doesn't mean they're not fighting a war. I know this plan is bad, Cassie, but we've got to think of the big picture." He looked at her and touched her shoulder again.

"Yes," Ax said calmly. "The Yeerk pool is a command and control centre. It is central to Yeerk military activity. They recharge there so they can continue their conquest."

"Not true," Cassie insisted, regaining her

voice. She leaned forward. "What about Tidwell, and others like him in the peace movement? They have to go to the pool because they'll die if they don't feed. For them, it's no different than eating."

"The peace movement Yeerks are a small minority," Jake countered coldly. "We can't really consider them, except maybe to warn them."

"Not consider them!" Cassie repeated, disbelievingly.

"What if your brother's at the pool when the gas explodes?"

Jake looked at his hands. "I guess it's a sacrifice I have to deal with, in order to protect thousands more," Jake said, his voice now expressionless.

"Jake, I don't believe you!"

"You should," he said, looking back to Cassie. To me. "Besides, family involvement doesn't really come into play here. It can't. The Yeerk pool is a target. End of discussion. It's not like we're bombing a bunch of innocent people at the mall on a Friday afternoon. . ."

Again, I looked at the people all around us. Families, couples, kids like us. Enjoying themselves. Here to see a movie, meet their friends, shop for clothes. They'd done the jobs they had to do at work or at school. Now was their chance to relax. Have fun.

Cassie looked around the food court, too, and then back at Jake.

"Isn't it?"

That's pretty much when Cassie decided she couldn't do it. She decided to sit the mission out. I admired her. I even thought about pulling out myself.

But who would be around to figure out Taylor? Who would be there to watch for sabotage? I'm not really sure how or why we decided I was the best one for the job. But I decided to do it.

Early that evening Ax and I flew together, an owl and a red-tailed hawk, high up into the night sky so we could get a good look at the place before we landed. We wanted to be as sure as possible that we weren't flying into a trap. The natural gas pumping station came into view.

<The coast appears to be clear,> Ax relayed. <Why do humans refer to the "coast" when talking about a precarious situation?>

<I don't know,> I said. <It's just what we say.>

There wasn't anything within a kilometre of the structure. Just trees and bushes. I swooped low to check out an abandoned van left a hundred metres or so from the pumping station. No hidden group of Hork-Bajir waiting for us.

The pumping station was pretty small, just a square building, about as big as a house.

Security lights brightened it like a baseball stadium just before a night game. The lights made my hawk vision work almost as well as the owl's. Through the few windows, I could see a maze of pipes.

We landed on the ground behind a line of thick bushes. It's hard to land directly on the ground. It's easier when you can grab on to something with your talons. I skidded a little. Ax was right behind me.

<Well, Ax-man, I guess it's now or never — and, boy, do I wish it was never,> I said.

I morphed and Ax demorphed. Two identical blue aliens began to sprout from the bushes. I like the way Andalite morph feels. It's about strength and agility. A focused yet playful mind. An unwavering optimism that's invaluable when you're up against pure evil.

We finished morphing and Ax trotted up beside me. His main eyes studied me. His stalk eyes scanned the area around us. Then, suddenly, his tail snapped and zipped across the blue-and-tan fur on my chest.

<Hey, watch it! What are you doing?>

<I am removing portions of your fur. We call it "*unschweet*". I believe you say haircut. I must make you look less like my genetic double.>

<Fine,> I said. <But be careful. No razor burn.>

<When an Andalite warrior is reprimanded

for his conduct,> Ax continued, <a superior officer removes some of the offender's fur so that the transgression is not soon forgotten. In the ritual of *unschweet*, the wrongdoer is not punished in the traditional sense. He must live with the constant reminder of his error and the scrutiny of his peers. As his fur grows back, he is slowly redeemed until, finally, the incident is laid to rest and the warrior is whole again.>

<I've had bad haircuts before but I never knew what to call them. So Ax, do I deserve *unschweet*?>

<No,> Ax answered. <But it is the only way I know to cut fur. Sorry.>

<It's cool. Let's just get this over with.>

We walked cautiously towards the pumping station, staying out of the brightest lights and watching our backs with our stalk eyes. A tall fence topped with barbed wire ran all around the structure, but the rear gate was open a crack. Someone was expecting us.

I pointed a slender finger towards the gate.

Ax moved out in front. An eerie squeak cut the still air as we slipped through the gate.

We moved quickly towards the shadows that clung to the wall of the building.

"Evening, boys."

She stepped out of nowhere. A dark, human form with a voice that sent chills down my spine.

It was Taylor.

"Nice to see you. I've been waiting."

She'd been there the whole time. I couldn't believe it. We'd been so careful. How had we missed her?

She was wearing dark leather from head to toe. Tall boots that came up to her knees. Her long blonde hair was tucked into a high leather collar. It was a new look. Goodbye preppy. Hello soldier. We stared.

"I'm not here to be gawked at. I'm here to deliver a present," she sneered. "I know how much you both like Taxxons. I found a choice one — very big, very mean — to show my appreciation for your help. Follow me."

She disappeared into the pumping station. Ax followed her. I followed Ax.

We had to duck low to clear some of the pipes. The noise was unbearable, a constant clanging that made my head hurt. Taylor descended a twisting metal ramp into the basement. We followed, stepping carefully on the slick surface.

Downstairs it was considerably darker, though there were fewer pipes. Taylor stopped in a corner of the room and gestured to an iron handle protruding from the smooth concrete floor. Then she backed up, leaned against the wall, and crossed her arms over her chest.

"He's in there."

Ax and I looked more carefully. The iron handle was attached to a large slab of concrete set into the floor.

<This is it,> I said to Ax. Trying to forget I was in the same room with the monster who'd come close to destroying what little peace of mind I'd ever had. I bent down and grabbed the iron handle with my relatively weak Andalite arm. It didn't budge.

<I will assist you,> Ax announced. Together we pulled with all our strength. The slab rose out of the floor. With great effort, we set it to one side. A snort from below sent us both jumping back.

"How cute," Taylor said. "You're scared."

<We are not frightened,> Ax said coldly. <We are cautious.> He stepped up to the hole and peered inside. <I see no sign of the Taxxon.>

Taylor tilted her head to one side and looked at Ax mockingly. "Then go get him, silly."

The cavern was dark. I could just make out the bottom, about three metres away. It seemed to curve slightly. I guessed it was a tank, an old fuel storage reservoir or something.

The last thing I wanted to do was jump into a dark tank with a Taxxon waiting to eat me.

Again, Ax led the way. If he wasn't fearless, he was putting on a good show.

<It is a long way down, Tobias,> he called from below. <Bend your knees on impact.>

Taylor was watching, her beautiful face wearing the look of perpetual disdain she'd perfected. I couldn't let her see my fear. I hopped over the edge and braced for impact.

WHAAAMMM!

My hooves hit hard on the concrete bottom. Damp darkness enveloped me. I could just make out Ax at my side.

<Where is he?> I asked. <What if there's no Taxxon at all? What if it's a trap?> I thought of the others waiting outside, hidden in various morphs, watching. They were ready to storm the place if we got into trouble. But how long would it take them to reach us? I looked up and imagined being sealed in the tank. But then I remembered that Taylor couldn't lift the cover alone.

Or could she? How strong was that artificial arm?

It didn't matter. No. Between the two of us, Ax and I could probably come up with a few morphs that would get us out. But that comforting thought came too late to stop my hearts from racing. We stared into darkness, searching for the Taxxon.

Before he found us.

Ax moved forwards and disappeared. I strained to catch sight of him in the blackness. I saw slight movement to my right.

<Is that you, Ax?> I reached out to make sure of where he stood and. . .

<Ahhhhhhh!>

Agony shot up my arm.

<Ax!>

The Taxxon bit down hard. A thousand razor teeth shredded my flesh and muscle. He didn't sever my arm and have a quick snack. No. He sucked with iron jaws. Pulling me in. Dragging me closer to his stomach.

I swung my tail blade, but lost my balance on the smooth, curved floor. My hooves skidded wildly as the vile mouth chewed. I was caught in a slow-motion wood chipper!

Glowing red eyes, inching towards me. . .

I whipped my tail blade frantically, slashing the blackness, missing the Taxxon. The force of his jaws would rip off my arm!

<Ax!>

FWAP!

Razor teeth withdrew and I stumbled back, clutching my mutilated arm. I looked up. Dizzy. Ill.

<Hurry,> Ax said. <We must move quickly. I fear I have mortally wounded the Taxxon.>

Stupefying pain throbbed in what was left of my arm. I backed away. I could feel a wet, sticky ooze beneath my hooves. The Taxxon's vital fluids were spilling across the bottom of the tank.

I bent down. Reached out my good hand and touched the Taxxon's side. His soft side heaved laboriously, up and down, as he struggled to breathe. Yes, he was dying.

I could see Ax in the faint light, already acquiring him. I began to demorph. When the transition was complete, I reached out a talon and placed it on the disgusting flesh.

I could feel life draining from his body, and the firm folds of bloated tissue collapsing like a torn hot-air balloon. I concentrated on the acquisition.

Usually, you don't feel anything about an animal while you acquire it. This time, I sensed something. Fierce and elemental, like a scream of rage.

I finished acquiring the Taxxon's DNA. And realized there was something inside me unlike anything I had ever known.

Maybe it was just my own tormented mind at work. Or maybe it really was the DNA, screaming at me on some microscopic level. It was something terrible.

Something dangerous.

A tortured shudder moved the length of the Taxxon's body, from head to tail and back again. He shook for one violent instant, then stopped.

And I realized that he now lived only in Ax and me.

<It's sure enough about time, Bird-boy.> Marco's thought-speak greeted me at about a hundred metres. He was flying in, too, and was just as late as I was. It was dawn. We were both working hard to stay up in the cool air.

<Enjoying a leisurely breakfast while the rest of us get ready to work?> he continued.

Actually, breakfast was why I was late. This morning, the meadow had been unusually still. Not a field mouse anywhere. Kind of ominous, like they knew something I didn't. Like they knew it was better to stay at home.

I'd set out hungry, but along the way I'd

spotted a grey squirrel. It was bigger than I like, but food is all I think about. In nature, in my world, hunger doesn't just mean you'll be irritable in the car on the way to McDonald's. It carries undertones of death.

I'd dived, silent and swift. With wide-open talons I snatched it, unsuspecting, from the power line it was making its way across. The squirrel was heavier than I'd guessed. It yanked on my legs, sent me tumbling for the ground. I held tight. I even regained control, metres above the ground, flapping like mad to stay aloft.

But then, the squirrel's teeth pierced my leg. Sharp pain from the incision shot to my brain. I released one talon and let go of my would-be breakfast.

<Some of us actually have to work for our food,> I called to Marco. <But then, it's probably a huge deal for you to get the PopTart in the toaster.>

I landed gently on a tree branch. Marco was already demorphing. The others had gathered a few metres away. All but Ax, who was hiding in the thick grass, keeping an eye on the pumping station.

Jake had changed plans on Taylor at the last minute. He had to balance the danger of not having her accounted for as we dug with the risk of having our true identities discovered when we demorphed.

So Jake had let Taylor know, by email, that she couldn't come within a kilometre of the dig or the pumping station before 8:00 a.m. If she did, the deal was off. When she did show up, she had to stay with us as we dug.

She had agreed to Jake's conditions with an eagerness I found disconcerting. I didn't mention it to the others. I knew it was nerves.

I could see the manhole cover next to where the others were standing. It was partly covered with sand and stuck out above the ground about ten centimetres. This was a good place to work, with little chance of being seen. We weren't far from the pumping station but were concealed by trees and undergrowth on all sides. Taylor knew what she was doing.

The manhole cover was in a cul-de-sac, on the side of a gravel road that hadn't been paved. The concrete kerbs were in place and the gravel was carefully compacted a few centimetres below, ready for a layer of tarmac. It had been this way for a while. The site was supposed to be a new industrial park. But local residents didn't want the noise and the traffic, so construction had been temporarily stopped, leaving sewers and electricity, but little else.

"Your left talon's bleeding," Rachel said.

I didn't answer at first. I didn't feel like explaining. But Rachel's concern was genuine. It wasn't fair to blow her off.

<Breakfast sometimes bites back,> I answered.

"You're telling me," Marco broke in. "I was looking in the toaster to see if my PopTart was done and wham, the thing shot out and hit me in the eye."

<I'll be fine,> I said, looking Rachel's way.

"Let me have a look," Cassie said. She was still adamant about not going on this mission, but she wanted to know where we were digging.

In case we didn't come back.

Cassie being there was a little awkward. Maybe least so for me, I don't know. She wasn't there to wish us luck. And although Jake always gives us the option, it's really rare that one of us decides not to fight.

"You should morph to fix the cut," Jake said. "That thing's going to get infected. So I guess you'll go first."

I'd go first? That slammed me into the reality I'd been trying to avoid. I wasn't looking forward to the work that lay ahead. Or to the creature I had to become.

<The time is now 7:50.> Ax came trotting out of the bushes and stopped next to Jake. <The pumping station is clear, Prince Jake. We should start digging.>

Ax was wearing a Timex Triathlon timepiece around his front ankle. Rachel had picked it out for him. He feared that his internal clock might be thrown off by the power of the Taxxon morph. He and I were going to take turns wearing it while Andalite.

He moved briskly to the manhole cover, stuck the tip of his tail blade in the small hole intended for the crowbar and, with one swift, fluid twist of his tail, sent the twenty-five kilo steel cap tumbling through the air. It landed with dull resonance centimetres from Jake's feet.

"Smooth," Jake commented dryly. "You should work for the city."

I dropped from my perch to the edge of the hole. I could see that at the bottom of a three-metre shaft was a cylindrical chamber.

<I think I'll morph when I get down there,> I said. <Wouldn't want to be responsible for anyone spewing their breakfast.>

I hopped over the edge of the hole into the darkness, falling slowly, with partially open wings. A real hawk would never drop into such a tight space. I could feel the raptor's anxiety. I landed softly on the surface of the curved concrete.

"Take it easy, Tobias," Jake encouraged. "Nice and steady. If you have problems, we're here."

<Remember that you may not be able to control it like other morphs,> Ax instructed. <It might be too overwhelming to suppress. The few Andalites who have successfully used the Taxxon morph speak of becoming one with the

animal's nature, of channelling the violent energy. It cannot be stopped. But you can try to direct it. Use it, do not try to overcome it.>

"I'm right here, Tobias," Rachel called.

"Be careful." Cassie. "And . . . I'll see you guys later."

"Tobias. . ." Jake began.

<I can handle it, you guys,> I said, assuring myself as much as my friends. <I'll be OK.>